MOON MASTER

////

J.R. RAIN
MATTHEW S. COX

THE VAMPIRE FOR HIRE SERIES

Moon Dance
Vampire Moon
American Vampire
Moon Child
Christmas Moon (novella)
Vampire Dawn
Vampire Games
Moon Island
Moon River
Vampire Sun
Moon Dragon
Moon Shadow
Vampire Fire
Midnight Moon
Moon Angel
Vampire Sire
Moon Master
Dead Moon
Dragon World

Published by
Crop Circle Books
212 Third Crater, Moon

Copyright © 2019 by J.R. Rain

All rights reserved.

Printed in the United States of America.

ISBN: 9781794183742

Dedication

To Eve, the best ever.

1.

The crew was assembling.

Okay, admittedly it felt a bit like the Avengers coming together. Kingsley helped me with my bags, carrying them as easily as most men would carry a loaf of bread. Allison sat quietly with Tammy on the couch, laughing and holding hands like old friends. My daughter was maturing. I'd been hearing rumors of a boyfriend (and by rumors, I meant Anthony had been mercilessly teasing her), but I hadn't seen hide nor hair of the poor bastard, at least not yet. Tammy was, undoubtedly, nervous to bring him around. I reminded her that I had my ways to sniff him out. She rolled her eyes and told me they were just friends, but I could see it. Oh, yes, I could see it. As those eyes were rolling up, up, up, I saw something in them. Something close to love.

Just friends, my ass.

In fact, I seriously suspected Allison was getting the scoop even now, and probably promising not to tell me anything. The bitch. I'd torture the information out of her if I had to. Or guilt it out of her, whatever worked best.

And there was Anthony, only fifteen years old, but already over six feet. Yeah, he'd shot up like two or three inches in the past six months. His shoulders seemed to be broadening by the minute, too. He still walked like a kid though, slouched, slightly duck-footed. He picked up the habit of keeping his hands in his jeans pockets. He kept them in there when he walked, talked, and sometimes when he sat. It was, I suspected, "his look." Like all kids, he'd gotten stuck in a nowhere land trying to find himself, and so I quietly snickered, as he strolled by me, shoulders slouched, feet pointing out, hands in pockets. He looked like an extra on the set of West Side Story. He saw me giggling and shot me a look, but I kept a mostly straight face.

"What?" he asked.

"You're cute."

"Gross."

I snickered as he moseyed past me, and laughed a little harder when he tried opening the screen door with his hands still in his pants pockets. Amazingly, he did.

"He's so weird," Tammy said to Allison, who

promptly stated all boys are weird in an attempt to defend Anthony that didn't really sway my daughter all that much.

I shot Tammy a mental rebuke, reminding her he's her brother and she loves him and has his back. She reminded me that he had spent nearly an hour this morning popping zits. I reminded her that her boyfriend was probably doing the same, even now. She rolled her eyes, got up and stormed out.

Allison blinked at my daughter's dramatic exit and came over to me. "I take it the two of you had a telepathic fight."

"Not a fight. Just a lesson in manners."

"It's okay for siblings to bicker, Sam. Didn't you bicker with your brothers and sisters?"

I shrugged. "Yeah, maybe. But I'm also only close with one of them."

"Siblings don't have to be friends."

"But I want my kids to be friends. I want them to be like me and Mary Lou."

"And they probably will be. They have a bond that few siblings have. They have seen things, experienced things. Don't worry, they do have each other's backs when it really matters. In fact, you should be happy they tease each other. It comes from love."

"By the way, have you seen Anthony and his new look?"

"The hands in the pocket thing?"

I giggled. "Yes."

"When I was his age, I thought it was super cool to hook my thumbs in my belt buckle. I did that everywhere."

"You still do," I said.

"When a look works, it works."

"Do I have a signature look?" I asked.

"You fold your arms a lot and lean against things."

"What do you mean?"

"Like this."

She folded her arms and leaned her hip on the couch. As she did, she squinted her eyes and scanned the room.

"What's with the eyes?"

"That's what you do. You are always scanning, looking at everything. Nothing gets past you."

"You look like you're hurting yourself."

"It's not easy being you." She kept doing the 'me' pose.

"What's with the squinting?"

"You squint during the day, Sam."

"That much?"

"More, sometimes."

"I didn't know."

"Makes sense. I mean you do have a bit of a sun problem."

"Okay, you can stop doing that now."

"But I like being Sam Moon." She moved away from the couch but kept the same posture, arms folded, body leaning. Awkwardly.

"Such a bitch," I said.

"Look. I'm Samantha Moon."

"No, you're a bitch."

"Look at me, everyone. I'm a vampire with kids and a hunky man."

"Wait, what?" I asked.

"Oh em gee," said Tammy, sweeping out of the hallway. "You two are such dorks."

I slid in behind her, running my fingers through my hair and walking in the same uptight way my daughter sometimes walked. Allison did the same thing, and we followed her through the living room. "Look at me," I said. "I'm too cool for school."

"No one says that anymore, and I don't walk like that. All uptight."

"Sometimes you can walk a little... stiff," said Allison.

"Is that wrong?"

"Not at all," said my friend.

"But you think I can loosen up a little?"

"I think you are perfect," I added.

"Just tell me, please you guys. What should I do different?"

I think her eagerness might be related to this new boy.

"Just tell me how I'm supposed to walk. You're my mom. You're supposed to show me these things."

"But am I? I don't recall seeing that on the job description."

"But you think I can loosen up a little."

"Fine, maybe."

"Loosen up how?"

"Like this," piped in Allison. She walked away from us, hand on her hip, her bubbly butt rolling this way and that.

"Okay, not that loose," I said.

"Is that really how women are supposed to walk?"

"Yes," said Allison.

"No," I said.

"It's how *I* walk," said Allison.

The fact that Allison used to be a stripper in Vegas didn't come up often, but no one could keep secrets from my daughter so I left that alone, knowing she picked up that very thought.

"There's nothing wrong with the way anyone walks," I said. I stepped in front of Tammy. "Baby, my only wish for you is to be happy."

She brushed me off. "Yeah, yeah, whatever. Like this, Allison?"

Tammy pushed past me, knocking me aside with her hip of all things, as she sashayed through the living room.

"Perfect!" said Allison. "But more lift at the high end."

"Lift?"

"Like this..."

"No, like this," I said, and used my hip to knock Allison to the side... so hard she stumbled into the recliner.

"Sam!"

With Tammy giggling, I rocked the hip swivel all the way out the living room and through the front door and even down to the driveway, where I helped Kingsley load the minivan, certain that I could still hear my daughter giggling in the house behind me.

2.

We'd packed the Momvan to overflowing.

Kingsley drove with the seat pushed as far back as it could go, which still wasn't enough as he could have used another foot or two. Anthony sat in the front passenger seat, which left us girls in the back seat, where Allison and I did our best to get more boyfriend information out of Tammy. From the front seat, Anthony informed us that the boy in question was a loner at school and looked kinda weird. Tammy shot back that that was like the kettle calling the pot black. I let her know she got the saying backward and she let me know it was a stupid saying anyway. Pots weren't black and what the heck was a kettle anyway. She had a point.

The two-and-a-half-hour drive up the coast was mostly spent in silence; after all, my crew knew we went there on business, not fun. The Red Rider had abducted a young girl named Annie. It didn't help my emotional state that the missing girl was only ten years old... as far as I knew, substantially younger than any of his other victims. This kid was in a boatload of trouble, and only my daughter knew the full extent of the story, since she always looked into my mind. Allison knew a lot too, having unprecedented access to my head thanks to our months of blood exchange. As in, me drinking often from her finger, a transfer which gave me strength and also emboldened Elizabeth, something I hadn't been aware of at the time. The process also increased Allison's witchy powers, too. Now, it gave us a helluva one-sided telepathic neural connection. I say one-way, because her mind, by orders of her witchy triad, was closed off to me. Well, not me, but Elizabeth... who saw and heard everything.

But... Allison's access only went so far. I doubted she could have read the complete contents of Jeffcock's letter from my memory, or pieced together much more than anything I was currently thinking about. But what I thought about was surely enough... a little girl in terrible danger. The worst imaginable, quite frankly, and I had gone through it too, once, long ago, in another life.

So, yeah, I held some of what I knew back. There was just... too much to share with everyone, and I wasn't ready to share everything just yet... at least not all the personal details about my one-time father. And not with Annie still missing. Later, when the dust settled, I would catch them all up. Indeed, only Tammy, who had access to my mind 24/7, knew everything.

Kingsley, being an immortal, had no telepathic connection to my mind. Not all creatures are created equal, so to speak. Werewolves aren't too big on the telepathic stuff for example. Lichtenstein monsters have none as far as I know, and merfolk? I've heard theirs is the most powerful, but it comes with a cost—it's tied to sexual attraction. If someone isn't attracted to them, their telepathic powers are far weaker than mine.

For now, the others knew a young witch had been kidnapped and that the man—or entity—was a bad mamajama, and it would take our combined might to locate her in time. Anthony had asked, "in time for what?" But Tammy just shook her head. She knew the contents of the letter I had read, and knew that the Red Rider didn't just drink the blood of his victims, but feasted on them completely.

Troubled deeply and wishing like crazy we hadn't delayed even the amount we had delayed, I willed Kingsley to floor it. But he didn't. The man drove with surprising caution for an immortal. Then again, we did have my kids with us, neither of whom were immortal—I think.

I fidgeted, anxious, worried. A girl had been kidnapped by the very entity who had kidnapped me 500 years ago. My one-time father hadn't been terribly clear how old I—rather Daisy—was when she died. Only that they had lived together for 'many years' after her mother passed away. Some part of me wants to say she'd been around eighteen. It had taken me all this time to get a whiff of my magic back... and just as it would've returned to me in this life, I had been rendered into a vampire.

Not about me, I thought. *Not right now. Focus on little Annie.*

I worried terribly about a scared little girl somewhere out there. Undoubtedly, I had been scared, too, having been stolen away from my father and held in a cave, where a creature had proceeded to devour me. And not just my physical body, but my magic too.

Christ.

"Mom..." whispered Tammy next to me. She shuddered.

I knew getting out of people's heads was a problem for her. She heard all thoughts in an ever widening radius. And the closer the person, the more clearly she heard the thoughts. It was all she could do, she told me, to not go crazy. And even then, she still sometimes wondered if she'd already cracked. When she had said those words to me not too long ago, I had burst into tears. The words echoed my thoughts, and to think my precious little girl had uttered them too...

Ugh.

"Sorry, baby, "I said. "I will think of something

else."

"Thank you, Mom."

And so I smiled, preparing to bring up her boyfriend again—because inquiring minds wanted to know—but the little booger leaned forward and asked Kingsley why he hadn't asked to marry me yet. Stunned, I could only tip my hat to her. Kingsley, blindsided, nearly choked on his tongue. He cleared his throat a few times. Then cleared it again. We all waited for his answer.

"Marriage is, um, a big conversation, Tammy. I, um, yeah..." He cracked his neck. "It's something that, yeah, I've been..."

"Oh, quit yer stammering," I said, smacking his meaty shoulder. "She just said that to keep me from asking about her new boyfriend."

"He's not my boyfriend. Gawd!"

"Wait a sec, Sam," said Allison, leaning forward. "I think Kingsley was actually about to say something. Weren't you, big guy?"

"Well, it's something that's been on my mind." This time he most definitely didn't stammer.

I blinked. Then blinked again. Wait, what?

"*Really* now?" said Allison, her voice rising.

"Of course, Allie. I love Sam."

"Wait... holy smokes," said Anthony. "Is Mom blushing?"

"How is that even possible?" asked Allison.

"Oh, shut up you two. I have, like, blood. Of course I can blush. It just takes me, you know, longer to get there."

"You look so funny, Mom," said Anthony. "Your face is usually white like a ghost. Now it's all red and splotchy and weird-looking."

"I can't hear that enough," I said. Then took a deep breath. "Kingsley, maybe we can talk about this later? And Tammy, touché. That was a helluva conversation switcheroo."

"I know, Mom."

Truth was, we hadn't talked about marriage. And if we had, it certainly hadn't been a serious conversation. I knew Kingsley had been married before, twice actually, to a mermaid in Seattle, no less, who was still alive and working as a private investigator. And a first wife—a human wife—who had long since passed. I know I wasn't in a hurry to marry. Dealing with the devil, my kids, my new wings, demons, and the demands of my job certainly kept me busy. Hell, Kingsley and I were lucky to get a few nights together each week. But when we did, we took advantage of them...

"Oh, gross." Tammy cringed.

"Wasn't me," said Anthony automatically. "But I can't promise it won't be me the next time. Or the next. Or the next..."

"We get the idea," I said.

"Not *that*." Tammy pressed her fingers to her temples, eyes closed. "Mom was just thinking a really gross thought."

"A brief gross thought," I corrected. "And it's

not that gross. Or gross at all, in fact."

"Eew, mom. Just, eww. I can only throw up so much."

"What was the gross thought?" asked Kingsley and Allison in unison.

Tammy shivered. "Never mind..."

"A sex thought?" asked Allison, studying me. "Really? Here?"

"Mom's blushing again," announced Anthony.

"Well, I didn't mean to think it here."

"She was thinking about what Kingsley said—or almost said—and one terrible thought led to the next," said Tammy.

"*Really* now?" asked Kingsley, glancing over his beefy shoulder at us. I could almost, *almost* hear the collar of his shirt straining.

"Forget it," I said. "Let's get back to what you almost said."

"What did I almost say?" he asked, turning back around and facing forward, both hands gripping the wheel.

"Don't play dumb."

"But I do it so well..."

"Tammy," I said. "What did he almost say?"

"He almost said—"

"I'm not a fan of this game," grumbled Kingsley.

"Tell me about it…" Anthony rolled his eyes. "You have one single thought about one girl at school, and your sister is yelling at you from down the hallway."

"It's not one thought." Tammy scoffed. "It's like hundreds of them all day long."

"Well, that's *normal*," said Anthony. "I have *normal* thoughts."

"Sadly, you do." Tammy smirked. "Maybe more normal than others."

"Tammy," said Allison, "is there no way you can turn it off? The telepathy, I mean."

"None that I can find."

"Honey," I said. "Would you like for me to ask Max for some advice—"

"Actually," said Tammy. "I would like for you to ask you-know-who."

I paused, my breath catching. Yes, I knew who she was talking about. Intimately, in fact. Then again, not intimately enough that we've had long conversations. Long conversations tended to embolden the dark master within me. I didn't want to embolden her. I wanted her weak and forgotten.

"Yeah, yeah, Mom. But she might be able to help me."

"Help you how, exactly?"

"She might be able to, you know..."

And just like that, my daughter burst into tears. It was a good minute or two before Tammy got control of herself again.

"I'm sorry," I said, hugging her.

"It's not your fault. Not really."

"I know it's hard..."

"Mom... you have no idea. My thoughts... sometimes I don't know which are mine, or from whom or where the thoughts are coming from. Sometimes I just sit there with my mind spinning, my head full of noise, wishing I had the guts to just end it."

I gasped, totally not prepared to hear those words. Was my daughter actually considering suicide because of her remarkable gifts? Gifts bestowed upon her because of her close proximity to me? I knew she could hear my thoughts, but mercifully, she sat quietly in my arms... in Allison's arms too, who sat on the opposite side of her. We sat like that for a few minutes.

"The good news," I said, finally releasing her, "is that you used 'whom' correctly."

"What? Oh, Mom. You're such a dork."

But she giggled at that, and that was a sound I could listen to all day long, 24/7, on a friggin' loop.

I noted that Elizabeth had perked up. I knew this because I could feel an inky presence appear at the back of my thoughts, looking out from the shadows. Elizabeth, of course, had been a helluva telepath in her day, perhaps one of the strongest ever, as evidenced by her son's and my daughter's abilities. Max the Alchemist was as gifted as they came, but not even he, I knew, could turn it off. Could Elizabeth help my daughter? Would she help my daughter? And what would she want in exchange? I don't know, but I had to find out.

I'm going to need my head on straight when I

talk to her, baby, I thought. And it's not on straight. Not with Annie missing.

It can wait, Mom. And no, I don't really want to kill myself. I just need a break... just every now and then.

I patted her head and pulled her into me, which meant I pulled Allison into me too, since she was still hanging on from the other side. We ended up in a pile on my side of the van, and we huddled like that for the rest of the trip. I was in heaven, even if Allison was heavier than I would have guessed.

"Hey," she said.

Tammy giggled.

"And don't think I forgot about you, Mr. Kingsley Fulcrum," I said. "You have some splainin' to do."

He shook his big, shaggy head, and we all settled in for the drive to Santa Barbara.

3.

With the crew chillaxing at the hotel in Santa Barbara—two super-nice suites courtesy of Kingsley and his millions—I headed out alone to meet with the parents of the missing girl.

As I approached the front door of a modest family-style home with an immodest view of the Pacific Ocean, I considered my inheritance. Was I really the owner of a mansion? A dilapidated mansion, mind you, but a mansion nonetheless. The short answer was... yes.

Yes, I was.

"Wow," I whispered again. The full effect of my inheritance had been eclipsed by the letter from J.C. Yes, that's short for Jeffcock. And, yes, I refused to call my one-time father by his given name. I just...

can't.

Nope, nope.

J.C. it is.

Anyway, now that both the letter and the inheritance have sunk in, especially after many minutes of quiet contemplation in my Allison/Tammy pile in the back seat... yeah, wow. I owned a mansion. A big ass, haunted ass mansion.

Okay, maybe I *didn't* have words yet to express the shock.

I stepped up to the front porch, briefly admired the view of the Pacific Ocean it afforded, and realized all over again that this bastard, the Red Rider (as my one-time father had called him) had been abducting witches—young witches mainly—for the past five centuries.

Centuries.

Yeah, this piece of shit was going down. One way or another, he was eating the Devil Killer. And if the Devil Killer couldn't get him, I would figure out another way. But I suspected the Devil Killer would do the trick. Oh, yes.

Earlier, I had contacted Detective Sherbet to cross-check the information I'd been given in the Occult Reading Room. Not that I doubted what the angels and the Alchemist had revealed, but I needed some cold hard facts. Yes, a girl had been reported missing a week ago. The police in Santa Barbara were on it with all hands on deck. Sherbet had been keeping an eye on it himself, and, amazingly, had been tempted to call me if things went on for another day or two.

I'd asked what made him think of me, and he said it had been something in the missing person report. The parents had talked about their child being *gifted*, in touch with nature, magical almost. It had made him think of me. And it had made him suspect there might be a paranormal element to all this. I told him he had no idea. He'd asked how bad it was. I told him the worst. He asked if I would look into it. I had told him the child's guardian angel had beat him to it. He'd raised a bushy eyebrow (okay, I might have imagined that, since we were on the phone) and said 'Guardian angel?' I said yep and Sherbet asked why a guardian angel would need my services.

I told him I'd gotten involved because the abductor was a 500-year-old Inquisition executioner who concealed himself in the higher frequencies, beyond even where angels tread. Sherbet remained silent. I asked if he was still there. Sherbet grunted. I asked if he was okay. He grunted again. I asked if I should hang up. And he grunted a third time. But before I did, he said to call him if I needed anything, especially if I needed backup. He said he was always there for me. I told him he was a brave man, and he said *I* had no idea. Well, I had *some* idea.

Now here I was, standing outside the small but beautifully positioned home overlooking the glittering ocean, a home that had been wrecked, undoubtedly, with the disappearance of a young girl.

I took in some worthless air, centered myself, and knocked on the front door.

***

We sat in the kitchen dinette area.

Opposite me were a man and a woman who had seen better days. The home was cute, but the mood inside was dark. I found little if any spirit energy, which I considered as a good sign their daughter was still alive. Some believe spirits are bound to the place of death. I have discovered there are no rules when it comes to spirits. Some are bound because they believe they are bound. Others can flit about, coming and going. Most are just aspects of the soul... memories of the living, with the soul themselves having gone on to the afterlife. In the case of Danny Moon, he had fled the devil and sought refuge in my son, while an aspect of him had hung around an underground cavern. Long story.

The parents told me the police had just left, as had some of their friends, and that this was the first time in days they'd been alone. Except now that they were alone... they hated it because it seemed like, well, they might be alone forever. That their little girl might really be gone. And they didn't even know why they were telling me this. Who was I again? I'd eased their concerns with a few gentle suggestions. Except my suggestions weren't really sticking, so distraught were they.

Anyway, had I seen the spirit of a young girl in this house, I would likely have to give the parents the bad news that their daughter had passed. Then again, not all ghosts return to sit with distraught parents, especially if the corporeal body had been killed elsewhere. Some spirits were bound to certain places for reasons I could never quite understand.

Although the parents weren't out of the woods, *not* seeing her spirit gave me some hope.

I had introduced myself at the door, and they had been confused at first, until I gave them both the impression that it was okay to let me in, that they could trust me, that I was here to help. I wasn't sure if my impression/suggestion would push through the pain and fog, but it had, temporarily. Wordlessly, they had stepped aside and showed me into the kitchen.

Allison had wanted to come, but I asked her to stay behind at the hotel. I do my best work one on one with a client, even though these people weren't paying clients. Had they known the child's guardian angel, among a legion of other angels, had sought my help, they would perhaps both be elated and dismayed. After all, it was never a good sign when your guardian angel loses track of you.

I pushed a little harder inside the mother's mind... and still found no cracks. Just confusion and pain and suffering and loss and hate and fear and more hate and more fear. Wow, Rita was looping. I gave her a small suggestion to calm her down a little, and she settled into her chair and cried softly into her hands. At least the looping stopped.

I saw in their thoughts what I wanted to see: loving parents who cherished their unusual child. They called her their "forest baby" because she was always out in the woods, always sitting with her bugs, which she particularly loved, to the chagrin of her mother. "No, the bugs are important, mama" I heard her say, over and over again, in her mother's mind, a repeating memory. Rita hated herself for coming down on her child who loved nature so much that she even loved the bugs and spiders and worms, and would sit with them and protect them and help them when she could. This kid who wept when mosquitoes and flies got caught in webs, and ran out into the rain to help the flooded earthworms find their way back home again.

Truthfully, I was with the mom. *Eww.*

But something also pulled at me, too. Nearly forgotten memories of being a kid and being enchanted by all of nature, too—yes, even the bugs. My adult self didn't like bugs. My child self... well, she was a different story. I grew up in the forests of the Pacific Northwest. California, to be exact. I had been a tomboy, and my parents were straight up hippies. We had lived simply, sometimes even living off the land itself, growing and stealing crops... even while Dad grew a distinctly *illegal* crop. At any rate, I have many memories of my endless fascination with the forest critters, with insects among them. Mostly, I had been fascinated with owls, of all things. We had a number of them in the forest around us, and I would sit for hours and watch them high up in the tree branches, their heads turning nearly 360 degrees, their hoots filling the forest. I found their sheer size fascinating. Big as eagles, but with faces unlike any other avian. Little did I know that someday I would turn into a flying creature myself, as a strangely flat, stub-nosed entity that I had at first assumed to be a giant bat, only to learn it was closer to a dragon. Now, I wonder if it—if Talos—looked, in fact, like the great grey owl in the Pacific Northwest. Hard to say. Then again, how could I have known that someday Talos would be in my life?

My one-time father, J.C., informed me that I'd spent a period of my existence not in this world, but somewhere else entirely, on a world where dragons flew. It had been, perhaps, the strangest thing of all in his letter to me. My one-time father who had mastered seeing beyond the veil, so to speak, the lives between lives. And if I read J.C.'s letter correctly, I had mated with another such flying creature.

Talos, I was sure of it.

What were the chances that the creature I had mated with would be the very creature I turned into? I didn't know, but there was something going on here, something I would get to the bottom of soon enough.

Meanwhile, Annie's parents seemed as loving as two parents could be when faced with a child who didn't play video games or text her friends or watch cartoons. They knew she was different and they loved her uniqueness, even if they didn't know what to make of it. Most importantly, they weren't hiding anything nefarious, which I never truly suspected, nor was it mentioned by the child's guardian angel.

"Who are you again, Miss?" asked Rita.

"Samantha Moon," I said. "I'm a private investigator in Orange County."

"Where in Orange County?" asked Gene.

"Fullerton."

"A long way from here," he said.

"I feel like you told us, but my brain... it's a bit foggy. Can you tell us why you are here again?" asked Rita.

"I'm here to find your daughter," I said, saying the words a helluva lot more confidently than I felt them.

"Who... who hired you again?" asked Gene, frowning and looking at his wife.

They were, of course, both still feeling the effects of my light suggestion, a suggestion which I never intended to stick for long.

I considered how to answer. I considered giving them the suggestion that, in fact, I had already given the answer, and that they were satisfied with the answer. But this was their daughter, and she was in trouble, and I wanted them to know what had happened to her, and why, and what I planned on doing about it. If they couldn't handle it, well, I could always wipe their memories clean of it.

But as I opened my mouth to begin the tale of witches and guardian angels, of the Inquisition and the Red Rider, I closed it again. Not only would the story take too long—and time was of the essence—I discovered I just couldn't get the words out. Not to this couple, already so broken. And so I told them that I was a specialist in finding the missing and that the police had reached out to me for help. That I was on the department's payroll (which I was, even though it was the wrong department). I told them just enough to satisfy their curiosity, and I followed it all up with a simple suggestion for all of this to be believed and accepted without question.

With that done, I asked, "When was the last time you saw your daughter?"

"A week ago," said Gene.

"Seven and a half days ago," added Rita, and I could imagine the terrible dread she was going through, since I had been through something similar a few months ago with Anthony. That said, my son hadn't been kidnapped for longer than a half day.

Half a day is a half day too long.

And she had been dealing with it for over a week.

I was tempted to ease her pain with another suggestion—both of their pains—but felt doing so was unfair, denying them their natural parental reaction. Five centuries ago, my one-time father had found me dead in a cave weeks after I'd disappeared. He'd mentioned I had been recently killed and consumed. By his judgment, I had been killed a week or two after my abduction. Why the Red Rider waited, I didn't know, but if this was truly his M.O. then we might still have hope.

"Tell me about the day she went missing," I said.

They did, and, admittedly, their tale had me sitting up and taking notice.

Rita began. "Our daughter was—I mean, is—different. Why do I keep doing that? That scares me." Her hubby patted her hand. "She played in the woods more than she played at home. Among the many things she claimed—Gene, you tell her."

He looked at me hesitantly and I sent him a small nudge, reminding him I was here to help, I was a friend, and that I was charming AF.

He sat up beaming, leaning toward me, and I promptly eased back on the charming AF part. Oops, too much charm.

"One of our daughter's quirks, if you could call it that, is that she claims to talk to... fairies," said Gene.

"Interesting."

"Of course, we don't really believe her—"

Rita jumped in. "We thought it was, you know, like having an invisible friend or something."

Gene nodded. "She claimed to talk to them all the time."

As they spoke, I had the briefest flash of a memory, of something small and beautiful coming up to me in the forests back home when I was a kid, something that buzzed around my head, paused... smiled at me and left. I ran home and told my mom all about it. She had laughed at me and told me I had been in the sun too long, and that if I kept making up stories I wouldn't be able to go out into the forest alone anymore. It had been the last time I had seen such a creature. Or had I seen it? It seemed more dream than memory. I had, I knew, been a budding witch in this life, finally regaining my powers which had been consumed by the Red Rider, powers that had taken several lifetimes to re-ignite, so to speak.

Gene continued, "According to her, they were everywhere... in the garden, in the forest."

"Have you ever talked to anyone about this?" I asked.

Gene and Rita shared a glance. "No. No one. We were embarrassed. Quite frankly, I have no idea why we are telling you now."

"Because you trust me and know that I am here to help."

"Yes, of course," they said together.

I looked at Gene. "Go on."

"We thought her talking to fairies and 'forest spirits' was just a phase until... well, until I saw one myself."

He had been sitting in his car, relishing a few minutes of quiet after returning home from work. He was a film agent in Hollywood, and although the job sounded glamorous, it took a lot of his time, and sometimes he would just sit in the driveway here with the windows down, listening to the wind and birds and squirrels, trying like hell not to look at his muted phone. He had dozed off... and awoke to find his daughter emerging from the woods behind the house. The family lived high up the mountain range just behind Santa Barbara—a range I should know the name of but didn't. The woods behind the house certainly didn't compare to the redwoods I grew up with, but the trees here were numerous enough, though a bit stunted, and only a few dozen feet tall, rather than the hundred plus in Northern California.

Still, a woods is a woods, as long as there were trees and underbrush and wildlife, of which they had plenty here. He and his wife had long since quit worrying about little Annie being alone in the woods behind the house. First off, the family owned most of the land behind the house—he had opted to buy land, rather than a bigger home. And second, Annie had proven herself to be a rather competent outdoorsman, never mind the hundreds of crazy stories she returned home with, many of which they had asked for her to keep to herself, so strange and surreal and sometimes alarming as they were. Hearing about her talking to fairies was one thing, but hearing about the wood spirits teaching her magic spells was another. They had nearly put a stop to it until she had assured them she would speak of it no more, and she hadn't.

But when he had seen her emerge from the woods, he had seen the glowing lights following her... many lights, in fact. And he saw... really saw... what they were. He had sat in his car, mouth hanging open, as tiny, human-like figures with wings trailed behind her and around her, while she laughed and spun and twirled her way out of the forest. Never had he seen her so happy, and never had he been so terrified. He watched his daughter reach their back door—his driveway was positioned in such a way that he could see the backyard and the slopes of the mountain behind. There, she had held out her hand and kissed each of the flitting fairies as they had landed one after another on her palm. They rose up in a vortex of light... and shot back into the forest. Now alone, she had taken in a deep breath, smiled, and gone inside.

They didn't have many rules with their free-spirited daughter, but one of them was to come home before sunset, which she always did, every time. That is, until eight nights ago.

When the sun had set and Annie hadn't returned home, the search for their daughter had begun immediately. Mother and father had scoured the woods, going to all her known haunts. Although they didn't find evidence of their daughter, they had come across an unusual amount of wildlife. Finally, the police were called. The evidence was scant. Other than horse prints, which seemed to appear out of nowhere and disappear again, there was no indication of foul play.

I didn't tell the worried parents that their daughter had likely been kidnapped by a magic-eating immortal Inquisitor. Or that her fate would likely be the same as the hundreds of other young witches... to be consumed completely... the fate one of my former incarnations suffered hundreds of years ago.

Instead, I gave them a shot of optimism, told them I would do my best to find her, and headed out into the woods behind the backyard, wondering like crazy what the hell I was going to do next...

4.

I found myself recalling my one-time father's letter... and his search for me.

Turned out, I hadn't been all that far away. By my judgment, within about a fifty square mile radius. That J.C. found me at all is a credit to his perseverance. That he almost—almost—got to me in time is, perhaps, one of the greatest misfortunes of them all. My murder would lead to his search for my killer... a search that would span centuries and end in futility. Not only did my one-time father not find the Red Rider, he'd lost his immortality with a silver bolt to the heart. And with his death, as with all immortal beings who discovered immortality is merely for the lucky, he lost his chance at heaven and rebirth.

No, not futile, I thought, as I headed out along a

well-worn trail that led from the family's backyard. He left behind his love for me, and that was something I would treasure forever.

True, he might have been re-absorbed into the Is-All-Of-All, but his love would live on. Additionally, via his letter to me, he had laid out a foundation from which I could find the Red Rider. I don't think he ever intended for me to continue the search. If so, maybe he didn't know me very well after all.

No, I thought. He knew me very, very well. He knew I would take up the mantle.

After all, having been a victim of the Red Rider myself, I had a connection to the bastard. How I accessed that connection, I hadn't a clue. That it even existed within me was strange as hell. Which led me to wonder: did the murderous bastard have access to me as well? I doubted it. After all, he had consumed me long ago... not the other way around. As terrible as it sounded, I had become a part of him. I could access that part of me within him, just as Jeffcock accessed that part of him (his blood) that was a part of me... and spy on me as he saw fit. According to his letter, he hadn't spied too often. Truth was, I didn't care if he had. He was my one-time father and he had given up heaven for me. If watching his daughter with her family gave him a small amount of joy, so be it. Besides, it hardly mattered now, with him long since dead.

The sun had set about an hour ago, and I felt the

vibration of life pulsating through my body, the tingle of power and strength and invincibility. The way I felt now made me confident I could take on anyone. Even the Red Rider, whatever the fuck he was.

Be careful, child, came an oily whisper in the back of my mind. *This entity feeds on magic for a reason.*

I stood in the backyard at the top of a clearing. A ring of stunted trees arched around me.

He is a wizard. I know that.

He is a sorcerer, Sssamantha. The darkest of the dark. Put another way, his evil is unheard of, his abilities unknown. He treads where even angels cannot go.

The upper dimensions.

Yesss. Why do you think your goody-goody father had such a terrible time finding him?

I don't know. Why?

The Red Rider, as he is now called, was on other worlds, other planes of existence, far, far, far from here.

Then why does he return here?

To feed, Sssamantha. The pickings are easy, and the beings here are three-dimensional.

You lost me.

The beings here are physical. Higher up, from the fourth dimension and onward, the beings are energetic. He comes here only long enough to feed, and then he flees again.

Great. And how and why should I trust you?

Does it feel like I am speaking the truth?

I ignored her. I didn't want to get into debates with her. Not now, maybe never. Mostly because she *did* seem honest at that moment. She had far too much access to all of my thoughts. She knew all my hopes and dreams and fears and worries. She also knew what triggered feelings of warmth and trust, which meant she also knew how to manipulate such feelings. That said, her words made sense, and I didn't have a ton of reason to doubt them. But I would always doubt the woman sent to possess me, specifically to take me over and to release all sorts of hell on earth. Um, yeah. Hard pass.

Still, the woman was undeniably old, clever, and versed in the darkest of magicks. Additionally, she had a vested interest in keeping me alive, on the off chance that I eventually gave in and allowed her control over my body.

Emphasis on *off chance*.

The path before me could have been a game trail. I also suspected the path was well worn thanks in part to Annie's daily trips into the woods to visit her forest friends. I once had forest friends, too, and being here now further awakened memories I'd long dismissed as wild flights of the imagination... or dreams.

Which made a kind of sense. Turned out, a lot of these young witches were instinctively drawn to nature, as witchcraft, in general, was an earth-based magic. In this life, I had been drawn to the dense woods behind—and around—our home, as we had lived mostly off the grid. I, too, had heard the whisperings of the forest. I, too, had felt the pull to explore further and further. But I had never been taught spells by wood spirits or communed with animals, and I suspected I knew why. My magic was not up to par yet. It had been depleted by the Red Rider, and it had taken many lifetimes of reincarnation for the magic to build back up. This life was supposed to have finally awakened the magic within me. I suspected I would have needed Allison's help... and the help of the spirit, Millicent. But I was never given the chance. I had been turned before the trifecta could form.

Yes, yes, came a voice from not-so-deep within. *So you missed out on being a witch. You gained immortality, Sssamantha. You gained other powers too... powers you're only now just discovering. Look at all that you can do.*

She had a point, and she was also far more emboldened than I was comfortable with. Without warning or words, I tamped her down deep and threw a heavy mental sewer lid over the hole I imagined her in. And tossed a boulder on top of the lid for good measure.

Then I headed deeper into the woods.

5.

The woods here were... cute.

Meaning, they weren't *real* woods. There was nothing deep and dark about them, despite the sun having long since gone down. Then again, not everyone could see the flowing, glowing light filaments like I could. Still, this had nothing to do with light and everything to do with space. The area had plenty of empty ground cover and only a smattering of brush mixed between the twisted coast live oaks and bushy California pepper trees. I also recognized a few bottle brush trees, since we had one in our backyard. But that was the extent of my tree knowledge. Scratch that... I spotted a eucalyptus tree, and a damn big one at that. I headed over to it since it was sort of the king of the mountain, so to speak.

Maybe someday I would memorize every tree species, you know being immortal and theoretically having all the time in the world. Maybe I would learn a few languages as well. Might as well become a black belt in karate—and a black belt in every other discipline as well. Explore every country, too. With all the time in the world on my hands, there was nothing I couldn't do.

Maybe I'd get around to that stuff when the kids were in college. At this moment in time, I didn't have the luxury to sit around memorizing trees or practicing jiu-jitsu. I had to bring home the bacon... and I had people to help. Clients, mainly. But clients were people too.

I had to consider the off chance that Annie's guardian angel, who technically hired me, guided me to find this big eucalyptus tree. Something certainly pulled me toward it, and the last time I checked, I didn't have any clairvoyant ability. That was Allison's gift. Then again, I distinctly recalled having such a sense of 'knowing' when I was younger. Heck, it even seemed to be getting stronger as I matured... which is why I didn't doubt that I'd been heading toward a life of witchery.

But the hint of psychic ability had stopped, the instant I woke up that day in the hospital, with wounds to my neck after the world's worst jog, ever. No, not the worst. I could have ended up dead. But I had died, in a way. My past was dead to me, and a new life, of sorts, had begun.

Why was I missing my past life so much these days? I didn't know, but I had reached the big eucalyptus tree. Big was an understatement. This sucker was epic, rising high into the air, its branches swaying and rustling in a wind I couldn't feel. Almost as if it were speaking to me. Maybe even saying hi. Either that, or I really had gone nuts.

Speaking of nuts, I saw my first little light. It appeared from behind one of the upper branches and drifted down toward me. Then another appeared. Then another.

Then hundreds of them showered down around me.

"Sweet mama."

6.

I had seen such lights before... on an island in the Pacific Northwest. Skull Island, no less. No, King Kong didn't live there. At least, I didn't think so.

Of course, there hadn't been this many lights, but the size and shape were similar; that is, about as big as marbles and glowing white. They hovered, rising and falling on wind unfelt, on waves unseen. They almost seemed to be breathing as one, in and out, in and out... expanding, contracting, expanding, contracting... even as their numbers continued to increase the closer I came to the majestic tree.

The lights above and around could have been stars... that is, if the lights had remained stationary, which they didn't. They flitted and swirled and disappeared and reappeared. At times I sensed a sort of substance—a hint of tiny shapes—within the lights, but I couldn't see them, not really. Mostly, the lights sparked and faded. Curiously, they gave off a high-pitched whining that reminded me of downed power wires. If I had to guess, I would guess it was the sound of hundreds of fairy wings flying at once.

I could come up with no other explanation, despite not being able to see what, exactly, the white lights were composed of. Fairies, I suspected, only revealed their true selves to the innocent among us. Adults were not so innocent. Vampires were the least innocent of all. We literally had blood on our hands... and lips.

The bright lights were a sort of consolation prize... an acknowledgment of their existence, without a full reveal, so to speak. The question was... why would they reveal even this much to me?

My daughter claimed she could hear the thoughts of the fairies around our home. No, I hadn't known there were fairies around our home, and, yes, I had written off her claim. Perhaps she had sensed my dismissiveness because she talked of the fairies less and less. That's the thing with the little magical winged folk... they needed belief, I suspect or why bother?

The wind picked up, swaying the branches overhead, and the bright lights before me, too. The sight of them picked at a nagging sense of déjà vu. A half-memory came to me—I was eight or nine and wandering the woods behind my childhood home at night, probably headed to the big farm down the road to steal some vegetables. Out of the corner of my eye, I saw a speck of light gliding over the thick ferns. At first, I probably mistook it for some kind of firefly, but it was too large. I veered off the main path and followed the light, laughing and giggling. It paused, and circled me once, twice, and the 'firefly' became a tiny woman smiling at me. She touched her nose with a miniscule finger, then flew over and touched my nose, smiled again, and darted off, flying higher and higher and disappearing in the thick branches above.

I told my mom—and she promptly convinced me that I'd dreamed or imagined it. Fairies didn't exist, she'd said. I had been asleep in the forest or had let my imagination run wild again. I allowed her doubts to sink in, to sway me. Maybe I hadn't seen the little lady. Maybe I really had dreamed it. I never saw the fairy again. I would have forgotten about the event altogether if my mother hadn't reminded me about it a decade or so ago. "Remember when you were convinced you'd seen a fairy in the woods, Sun Dance? You were so excited, bouncing off the walls. It was all I could do to calm you down. I still laugh about it sometimes."

Yes, she often called me by my middle name. Yes, she'd laughed at me again.

An inexplicable jealousy rose up within me that both Daisy and this girl Annie had been allowed to have this experience, but it had been stolen from me. First by circumstance, second by being turned into a vampire. I'd been destined to be a witch again this lifetime and... No. I can't be jealous of an abducted child. I'm *not* jealous of Annie, I'm... sad. Like someone stole my puppy. It made absolutely no sense given all the powers I have, but a surge of anger came out of nowhere at losing that connection to the fairies, to the Earth. Even at Allison blocking me despite knowing she *has* to. I've never given serious thought to what-ifs before, but in that moment, I held a distinct sense of wanting what had been taken away. Of wanting, quite frankly, to be a witch.

Aww. Poor Sssamantha. You'd rather play with fairies than be immortal?

Oh, go to Hell.

Hard pass.

The thing was... well, that wasn't sarcasm from Elizabeth, was it? She really did pity me and my loss of magic.

Of course, Sam. What little girl doesn't adore fantasizing about fairies? she asked. *The ones who can see them—witches—deserve to. Consider my lack of sarcasm a token of respect from one witch to another... especially one who's had her magic stolen—twice.*

Meaning me, of course. Stolen once in a former life by the Red Rider, and stolen again in this life when I was turned into a bloodsucking fiend. Then again, wasn't Elizabeth directly responsible for that second part?

She was. The bitch.

Anyway, I stared at the fairies—in my case, bright white lights—weathering an inexplicable feeling of sadness, like being the unpopular kid gazing from afar at the others having fun I'm not allowed to.

Right. Whatever. I couldn't dwell on that now. I shouldn't have been dwelling on it at all. Not once had I ever really felt any sense of loss about my magic, and—no, that's not true. I had in the past, but never this strong.

Something weird was going on, but couldn't waste time figuring it out until after I found Annie.

I stepped closer to the great eucalyptus tree, the lights parting. Some drifted behind me, and soon all swirled around me, a few gliding closer. I held out my hand and a number hovered above but couldn't make the commitment to alight. That's okay. The downdraft of their wings blew like cotton balls rolling across my skin, and it was so cute I found myself smiling despite the reason why I was out here in the first place. I had to find Annie before that *thing* did the unspeakable.

And with that thought, the lights before me seemed to shift as well...

In fact, they calmed dramatically. No more seemed to be appearing or disappearing. All were present, but present for what?

No sooner did I wonder that, than the lights shifted again, and not with the wind, since the air remained calm. No, they shifted as one collective entity, somehow, like a flock of birds in slow motion, or a school of fish turning as one... slowly and deliberately.

The massive tree stood alone in this section of the woods. The next closest was a copse of evergreens that would have looked sickly in the Pacific Northwest, but here, looked majestic and out of place. I knew evergreens did grow in Southern Cal, but generally high atop the mountain ranges, like in Arrowhead or Big Bear. I'd had a number of adventures in both places.

Here, we weren't quite high enough or wet enough for the true evergreen giants to take hold... but they were trying. Anyway, the eucalyptus cared little for its neighbors, having grown massive and wide, soaking up whatever nutrients and water it could find. Its whitish bark peeled away in places almost like a birch tree. Unlike a birch tree, its leaves were fragrant and a bit intoxicating.

Against the backdrop of this mighty tree, unencumbered and unchallenged by other trees, the fairy lights began to collectively take on a recognizable shape...

And that shape was... wings. The mass of faeries shifted, reshaping itself. A head appeared in the center of the wings. More lights formed legs—no, talons.

Still other balls of light rose up, adding detail and verisimilitude to the massive creation before me. The head became blockier, the neck thicker, the chest more stout and muscular. The wings, now flapping, looked unlike any wings of any creature I had ever seen... no, not true. They looked like bat wings, with its swoops and arches.

No, not bat wings...

Dragon wings.

The head continued to take shape as now nearly all of the fairy lights had been utilized to bring this glowing, three-dimensional, light-filled creation alive before me. And then I finally recognized the snub-nosed head.

Talos.

The wings beat faster and faster, simulating flight, and the mouth the creature—well, Talos— opened wide, and a great bellow of fairy lights burst out in a gush of simulated fire, and continued gushing out of the mouth, until all of them had been sucked up and through the neck and mouth... first the talons disappeared, then the body, then the wings, until only Talos's great head belched fairy fire, and then even that dispersed.

"You know who I am?" I asked. "You know what I am, and what I become?"

The lights danced and jigged before me in response. Surely, had I been able to hear them, I might have gotten a clear answer. I considered how the creatures knew what I was, and could only conclude that the fairies, clearly organized and of one mind, all knew what each and every other fairy knew, a sort of network of cute little fey minds... kind of the way angels all knew what each and every other angel experienced. A one-mind. Perhaps the fairies in my yard at home had communicated with these fairies...

Perhaps. But why had they shown me an image of Talos?

And with that thought, the swirling lights rose up again into the night sky, up, up, into a white vortex of living Christmas lights.

Or... yes... I think the fairies could also read my mind.

Either way, creatures of the hive mind or creature who could read my mind, they were trying to communicate something to me.

The lights shifted and formed another shape.

It was, of all things, a portrait of a man. I was sure of it. Yes, it had a distinct nose, eyes, chin... and short hair, and a... wow, they even formed a beard. It was clearly a man... and a man I found oddly familiar. But I couldn't place him.

"Is this someone I know?" I asked.

The head made of light nodded.

Wow. Weird. And kinda cool, too.

The nodding paused and some of the fairies split off from the fine details of the man's face and formed into a sort of hat. If I had to guess it was a straw hat. Wow, okay, something was clicking in my brain... but it didn't click all the way. Frustrating as it was, I couldn't place the man... and I think the fairies wanted me to place the man. Desperate to, in fact.

The glowing lights of the hat dispersed and drifted, reforming as... something over the man's ear. Right ear, to be exact. It was a cap, perhaps, or a scarf...

No, wrappings. A bandage. As if the man had hurt his ear.

Or was missing an ear.

Okay, yeah. Wow.

They'd created a portrait of Vincent Van Gogh.

Of course, it is well known that Van Gogh had cut off his left ear and had given it, wrapped up, to a prostitute "friend" in France.

But since Van Gogh painted *Self Portrait* using a mirror, the bandaged ear appeared on the right side of his head.

All well and good, but what the hell did this mean?

I didn't know, but the name Van Gogh had come up now for a second time in as many days. And not just come up... I had a painting that just might be a Van Gogh replica. At present, the glowing fairy eyes shifted to me, and the lips moved too. They moved over and over and over, the lips and jaw and even the cheeks moving in concert. How these fairies managed to move with such uniformed precision, I didn't know.

But there on the hillside, with a craggy mountain rising beyond, with the swishing of the eucalyptus tree high above, the glowing image of Vincent Van Gogh spoke to me, and I'm pretty sure I knew what he/it was saying, despite not being a very good lip reader.

He repeated, "Come to me."

Over and over and over.

And once I seemed to understand, the images dispersed and regrouped into Talos once again. Only this time, the lights didn't stay in place. The wings flapped, and the glowing creature took flight, lifting off the ground.

It turned in the air once, twice, then sped over my head... and shattered into a thousand bright points of light... and began winking out of existence one after another.

Except for one. It drifted down toward me like a falling star, to hover before me. I was reminded of a glowing dandelion... as I could see a hint of depth and detail, but not enough to know what I was looking at. Up close, it appeared round and strange and supernatural. That is, until it started shifting and elongating, and sprouting big beautiful wings and long legs, and shoulders and arms and elbows... and a sharp, knowing, snarky, cute little face. I couldn't tell if it was male or female... although I leaned toward female. It put its little hands on its little hips, nodded at me once, then promptly turned back into a ball of light and zipped through the trees high above. I was pretty sure that thing that gleamed atop its little head was a crown. A fairy princess. Go figure.

"Alrighty then," I said, and began removing my clothing. "I get the hint. Talos it is."

7.

Hello, Talos.
Hello, Samantha.
I hope I didn't take you away from anything important.
You only take an aspect of me away, Sam. I am still in my world.
With me.
Yes. We are together on our favorite ledge, looking down at the swirling mists and occasionally up at the myriad of flying forms.
And I can shift to this "me" aspect when I want to.
You could shift back and forth if you so choose.
How does one bounce between physical bodies?
How do you think, Sam?
I nodded the great beast's head. The flame.

But of course. And who's calling whom a beast?
Sorry about that.
No worries.
You did not just say no worries, I thought.
I did, the words culled directly from your mind. It is a good concept, truth be known, allowing oneself and those around you to worry not. Worry is never good, and giving oneself and others permission not to is a good reminder.

Okay, you might have officially given more thought into that throwaway line than, like, anyone ever.

There is a reason why the 'throwaway line' found popularity.

And how do you know it found popularity?

Because I can see the proliferation of it ricocheting through your thoughts, from TV to your friends, to your family and children.

I thought you didn't pry too deeply into my mind.

Prying is one thing. Seeing your mind light up with examples is another.

Very well.

I flew gently high above, but not too high. Few would see us against the backdrop of the darkening sky, and fewer still would see the giant shadow pass before the stars. In truth, I was keeping an eye out for cave systems in the mountains around us, as I knew my one-time father had found me in such a system. A deep pit within a cave. I suspected there was a reason for it... and I suspected it was part of the Red Rider's M.O.

Talos, what am I thinking right now in your world?

I haven't a clue, Sam. I'm not inside your physical body's head. I know as much as you do. I would suspect you aren't thinking very deep thoughts at all. Hold on... okay, as I look at you in my world, your eyes are wide, but calm. It does not appear that you are breathing, but neither do you need to breathe. You're sitting cross legged with your face lifted toward our sun. You appear at peace, calm, relaxed.

Am I naked?

Yes.

And you can be-bop between this body and your body on the ledge? Just like that.

Yes, Sam. Just like that.

You have two bodies?

One body, two aspects. More if I want.

But how?

Samantha, the great masters of your earth were capable of being in two places at once. More than two if needed. Summoning a temporary body is not a difficult concept for those who have lived as a race for millions of years and have mastered the physical. I am many thousands of your earth years old, and expect to live many thousand more. I will remain around until I am ready to give up this body and move on to other adventures. But I am in no hurry to do so. I enjoy my life. I enjoy my world, and I am enjoying reconnecting with you. Mostly, I enjoy helping you and watching your own evolution. If all goes well, we can be having these conversations for many hundreds, if not thousands, of years to come.

I knew Talos's kind had been evolved for as long as mankind had been on Earth, perhaps longer. They had quite the head start on us.

Talos, if you are in two places, why am I not in two places, too?

You are in a way, Sam. Your mind is here, and your body is there, with me.

But you are in two *physical* places...

It is all based on intent. Your intent was to become something more in this life. I accommodated this intent, but to do that, I needed two physical forms. One to give to you, to use to your heart's content. The other to watch over your teleported physical body.

Then which one is the real you?

That is a good question. One that might need more exploration than time allows. But, for now, I will say... I don't know. I feel equally at home in both.

I've watched Kingsley transform into another creature, and I'm pretty sure he didn't body swap from something in another world. Also, he's described his ex-wife transforming into a mermaid. His description is similar to the process he goes through... body thickening and elongating and fusing, stuff like that. But what I am doing with you is different. We are body swapping. Or mind swapping.

The answer lies in the nature of the being, Sam. It is in his nature to transform into the wolfman or into the wolf. Likewise, it is in the nature of the merfolk to transform parts or all of their body into an aquatic creature. However, as a vampire, it is not in your nature to transform into a giant flying creature.

Yet I do.

Indeed.

How?

New rules had to come into play. Luckily, you are not the first of your kind to make such a request, and my kind has accommodated your kind for many centuries. There are, like I've said, a handful of us who work with your kind here on Earth.

Talos, I thought, as we flew together high over the local mountain range. The Santa Ynez Mountains. I mentally snapped my fingers. I knew I would remember the name. Were we mated in another life?

We were mated, yes.

Were we in love?

Very much so. You were, quite frankly, the love of my life.

What happened?

Talos did not answer, and I continued flapping

his great wings steadily, confidently, powerfully. Finally, I sensed him coming back 'on-line' so to speak.

You died in my arms, Sam.

I sensed the emotion in his voice, but also the acceptance.

What happened?

An accident. A terrible misfortune. Debris fell from the sky, which has been known to happen. You'd only been at the flying game for a few decades and couldn't right yourself. I shot down to catch you, but even I was too late. You were badly broken and bleeding profusely. You didn't die immediately, and I held you in my arms until you took your last breath.

As he spoke, I tried to summon the memory of it, the feel of it, anything, but my death was mercifully lost on me.

How long ago did that happen?

A few hundred of your earth years.

Talos, how did you find me again? It can't be a coincidence that you are my dragon familiar, so to speak.

No. It's not a coincidence. Your one-time father, Jeffcock, wasn't the only one who could see beyond the veil as some call... and into the world of the energetic. Many of my kind possess this gift.

He remained oddly silent as I continued to flap his powerful wings, adjusting to the many updrafts and warm and cold blasts. Mountains were tricky places, wind-wise and flying-wise.

I deployed the tracking skill similarly used by your father. You could say there were two of us tracking you through space and time.

You loved me that much?

I still love you, Sam.

I...never knew. Were you ever going to tell me?

Perhaps someday. Perhaps not. Certainly, if the subject ever came up. Certainly, if the time was right.

But I didn't understand... we are so different now.

The love isn't physical. I find your human form repulsive.

Gee, thanks.

I sensed him smiling at me. *No, Sam. I am in love with the real you, your inner self, the part of your personality that has held as true now as it was when I first fell in love with you on my planet.*

How did we meet, Talos?

Country line dancing.

I snorted, and twin flames of fire shot from my nostrils.

Ouch, that hurt.

You're telling me. Fire is meant to be released through the mouth.

Sorry.

No worries. I heal rather quickly, too. And we met at one of our public harmonic gatherings.

What the hell does that mean?

A few times during our calendar year, we all come together to raise each other's vibrations, and that of our planet, through chants and prayers and various techniques we have learned over the millennia.

Wow, weird.

But intoxicating.

And I was part of such chants?

Of course. You were very much part of our society.

How long did I live on your planet, Talos?

Eighty-four of your Earth years.

And how long were we together?

About fifty of those.

Wow.

It might sound long by your standards, but by our standards, it was a flash in the pan. I had planned on being with you for many thousand more years.

And now you are, sort of.

Indeed, Sam. I'll take what I can get.

Talos, I said after a short while of silent flying, I have no memory of our prior life together... or memory of our love. I only feel love for Kingsley now—

Let me cut you off there, Sam. Our window for love has come and gone, I understand that. You were not long on my planet... compared to others of my kind. Nor were you meant to be. I had to understand why you were taken from me so early in our relationship.

To think I had a relationship with...

I couldn't finish it. I didn't want to insult him, but Talos knew my every impulse and innuendo, every conclusion, comparison and concern. When it came to my emotions, there were no secrets from the great flying dragon who had access to every part of my mind, for my mind was his mind, too. At least, in these few moments when we were one.

Strange to comprehend, I know, Sam. But just remember, my kind loves deeply and has been doing so for far longer than humanity had sense enough to build fire. Believe it or not, in my world, I am considered quite lovable.

I snorted at that, and inadvertently let loose with another stream of curling, snapping fire.

A lovable, fire-breathing dragon. Why not?

Not quite a dragon in a traditional sense, but yeah, close enough.

My first impression of Talos had been that of a giant bat, judging by the shape of the wing membranes. Then again, I could never get a good look at him, except the few times I flew past a glass building. Mostly, I saw him in the single flame in my thoughts... those moments just before I felt myself rush toward him. In those images, he looked dragon-like... but yeah, also different.

I am just me. Big, lovable me.

Oh, lord.

He chuckled lightly in my head. *I know now you*

chose to reincarnate among my kind for that brief cycle for a reason, Sam. I know that now, although I did not know it then, which left me hurt and confused and lost for far longer than I care to admit.

I'm sorry, Talos.

I know, Sam. Not your fault. I should have known. I should have suspected. You were, after all, so different. So fresh and new and interested in everything about our world. More than anything, you were interested in flight. Correction, you were enchanted by flight. You loved to fly more than anything. Maybe even more than me.

He was leading in to something... I could hear the emotion in his voice, even if that voice was in my head.

What is it, Talos?

You made a strange request for me as you, ah...

He trailed off, but I caught the meaning and the mental impression he gently provided.

As I lay dying?

Yes, Sam. You made a simple request, but it was one I took to heart.

What was it, Talos?

You asked me to find you, and to fly with you... again.

8.

When I could find my voice, I asked the highly-evolved, fire-breathing, badass creature what he knew about accessing the higher frequencies.

I see you were given a vision of the frequencies a few years ago, Sam. This vision is remarkably accurate.

I had been given such a vision while meditating high upon a rock on Skull Island in the Pacific Northwest. The vision was a blur of places and faces, sights and sounds, as I rose up higher and higher up the dimensions. Finally, I had stopped at what I had assumed was the highest level, and there I met a great, swirling, beautiful presence. Except, of course, I had no idea how I got there or how to get there again. Besides, I'm pretty sure that had all occurred in my mind and not in a physical sense.

Yes and no, Sam. Accessing the higher frequencies is as much a mental exercise as a spiritual.

Have you accessed the higher frequencies?

I have. The higher realms are where deeper learning exists. The higher realms are a retreat from the day-to-day life.

You vacation in the higher dimensions?

He chuckled softly. More like re-charge.

For how long?

Not very long. You see... the physical body begins to degrade in the higher dimensions. We stay as long as we can. Days perhaps.

What are the higher realms like? Do people live there?

People, animals, other entities, you name it. These dimensions are not very different than your own, Sam.

How far up have you gone?

To the tenth dimension.

What was that like?

Hard to say. I couldn't see much. Or hear much. Or experience anything of significance at all. Mostly, I experienced forms of light and drifting shapes.

I'm not sure I understand. Why couldn't you see anything?

Because my frequency was not harmonized with the higher dimensions. Like a dog whistle that's out of the range of human hearing, the sights and sounds were out of my range as well.

But I thought you guys were pretty evolved.

Compared to humans, we are. But we are only closing in on the fifth dimension, which has taken us tens of thousands of years to prepare for.

How close is humankind to moving into the fourth?

It is not for me to say, but I can theorize.

Theorize away.

Another hundred thousand years. Perhaps longer, perhaps shorter.

That's a long ass time.

Humankind has issues to work through.

Yeah, I guess. So how did you end up in the tenth dimension? And who the heck lives there?

A number of races, Sam. Each dimension is filled with entities who occupy them.

So there is a race of beings who live in, say, the ninety-ninth dimension?

Of course.

And the Creator resides in the hundredth?

That is the speculation. Truth be known, I have never met another entity who knows for sure. You would be the first. Well, you and your vision.

But it was just that, a vision.

I can see it in your mind. I have relived it often as I find it most beautiful.

When do you relive it?

When we fly quietly, or sit quietly. Not so much when we are battling lake monsters and body-hopping demons. I am fascinated by your experience with the Creator. Unfortunately, the memory of it is fading with time. Luckily, I have formed my own memories of it now. My memory of your memory. It was and is a beautiful experience.

These levels... it almost sounds like you climb up into them.

You vibrate into them by synchronizing your frequency with that of the dimension.

Of course.

It's a bit like your Star Trek *TV show. When the vibration of a level is achieved, one finds oneself in the level. But, of course, these are not levels, these are worlds, Sam. Full, functioning, complete, beautiful worlds.*

But where are they? In this universe? Other planets?

The universe is layered and multifaceted, expanding as needed, accommodating as needed. Our fourth-dimensional world would not be spotted by your astronomers, and it's not because we are located in another part of the universe. We are not very far from you. In a hundred thousand years, when your kind reaches the fourth dimension collectively, you will not be very surprised to see the planets nearby that vibrate at different frequencies, previously undetected. Even now, more planets come into view not previously seen.

And the fifth dimension has planets undetected by the fourth?

Yes.

My brain hurts.

Imagine creating this crazy universe.

My brain hurts again.

I know, Sam. It's my brain too.

Okay, fine. Then how does the Red Rider, who I can't imagine vibrates very high at all, escape into the higher frequencies, so far up that even angels can't find him?

The angels, as you know, exist in the fourth dimension. My guess is he's no higher than the fifth. Maybe the sixth or seventh. Or, for all I know, he's found a loophole that allows him to travel the frequencies at will, although I've never heard of that, and it is not known that such a loophole exists.

Ugh. Not sure that's helping me.

I know. I'm sorry.

Answer this: what must an individual human do to ascend to the fourth dimension?

There are many on your planet who periodically dwell in the fourth dimension, some for extended periods. Others have never returned, so ready were they to ascend.

Fine, who are these people?

Religious faith is the surest way to reach the next level up, at least from the third to the fourth.

The Red Rider was an Inquisition torturer and executioner. He started as faithful.

Until he embraced his magical nature. And it would be safe to say, his dark *magical nature.*

Still, I can't imagine a murderer and torturer

reaching a level only the most holy can reach. Talos, what is the fifth dimension like?

It is not very different from your world, in appearance. But there is no pollution, and no sickness and no crime. There is harmony. There are whole communities devoted to the arts, for instance.

I can only imagine what the 99th level must be like. Actually, strike that. If the fifth dimension is already nearly perfect, I cannot imagine how much more perfect the 99th is.

I cannot either. But they are nearly all creators, too. In fact, I would hazard to say nearly all of them are.

Okay, fine. Head hurting again. Back to the Red Rider, how does this piece of shit garbage slip into a nearly perfect fifth-dimensional world?

That is the rub, as they say. I do not know.

You said something about a loophole...

It's all I can think of, Sam. When magic is involved... there is always the possibility of other factors at work. It's just that one cannot trick the universe. Those who exist in the fifth dimension vibrate at the fifth dimension. Simple as that. No exceptions.

Except for the Red Rider.

Except for him.

What role do you think Van Gogh has in all of this?

Let me access your memory of the man.

I don't know much.

MOON MASTER

You know enough.
Fine. Access away.
Moments later, Talos said: *The painting 'Starry Nights' is remarkably close to the seventh dimension's night sky. Maybe all the way up to the ninth.*
I had to process that before speaking.
Did he journey to the seventh dimension, then come back and paint it? Or did he himself create the seventh dimension through his painting? As would a creator?
I had recently met such a creator, a young painter who had been possessed and compelled to paint visions of hell... and inadvertently created the latest incarnation of the devil himself. Let's hope *this* devil learned a lesson from his predecessor... and stayed far away from me and my family. After all, I still had in my possession The Devil Killer, a sword that was no joke. I used it once on him, and I would use it again. Though, that made me wonder if the dark masters made an error. They supposedly chose me—likely at Elizabeth's behest—specifically because they somehow knew I would wind up in conflict with the Devil himself, and kill him. Thus, the dark masters would be free of their only real fear… being hunted and dragged to Hell. With the Devil gone, they'd been set free. But, the Universe creates based on belief, so how could they not have expected another entity would reprise the role of the Devil? Destroying the physical incarnation of the Devil didn't instantly eradicate

humanity's belief in him. Surely, the dark masters would've expected another devil to eventually step in.

A stirring tendril of annoyance shifted at the back of my mind. Hah! Did the great and powerful Elizabeth make such an obvious miscalculation? Her displeasure grew to a dangerous level, so I clamped down hard on that imagined steel cover and made the mental rock sitting on it even bigger.

Back to more pressing matters though: how is Van Gogh important? Annie's life is literally hanging in the balance here.

Talos followed my thoughts.

Van Gogh is a mystery to me. But I suspect he had access to the higher vibrations, and painted them. Like you, he might have had visions of them.

But my vision wasn't that detailed. I only passed the various levels quickly, on my way up to speak to the Origin. Once or twice, I caught glimpses at the various dimensions, but nothing I could describe definitively. Lots of light and swirling images.

Sounds familiar...

Well, I guess kinda like Starry Nights, but certainly not to the degree of vibrancy, detail and color of the Van Gogh painting. I only experienced the briefest of hints.

Which would suggest that he didn't experience the briefest of hints, that he was given extended access to the dimension. I do not ascertain, through your somewhat limited knowledge of the man, that he was considered a holy master.

No. I may not know a lot about him—but I suspect he was more troubled than enlightened.

And yet he journeyed to the upper frequencies, Sam.

Are we sure about that?

Oh, yes. Scanning the other memories you have of his artwork makes this abundantly clear to me. Although many of his works depict the struggles and grind of the human experience of his time, they are superimposed against the backdrop of the elevated frequencies. In a way, Sam, he was showing humanity's full potential... and what is ultimately waiting for them. Not all of his paintings, mind you, but clearly many. Which suggests he was, at times, accessing the higher dimension, and at others, not so much.

If I recall, he painted Starry Nights while at an asylum in France. There was another painting at that time, something about a Wheat Field with Cypresses.

Ah, I see it there in your memory. Too bad you didn't recently peruse a book of his art before having this conversation.

What can I say? Three days ago, I was cleaning skid marks out of my son's underwear.

Luckily, your memory is serving my purpose well. As you know, I can access all aspects of your mind, and I see now that the painting you are referencing is, in fact, called 'Wheat Field with Cypresses at the Haute Galline Near Eygalieres' and I am absolutely certain it is a scene straight from the fifth dimension, a veritable snapshot. Indeed, your artist, Vincent Van Gogh, was traversing the frequencies with some regularity.

And yet it is doubtful that he was an ascended master.

Based on your knowledge of the man, doubtful indeed. A clever and troubled artist, to be certain. A man loved by his brother and mother, definitely. A man understood in his own time, not at all.

Which could be why he sought solace in another time... or another dimension.

He could seek it all he wanted. But actually finding it... and traveling there is another story.

Yet he did, somehow.

Of that, I have no doubt.

So what's going on here?

I suspect your Van Gogh is a creator.

How so?

In your memory of his paintings, I count no less than thirty-nine self-portraits. Why do you think he painted himself so often?

I don't know.

To answer, let me ask you a question: what happened when the writer Charlie Reid wrote you into his World of Dur story?

I was able to step into it... to live in it. I became, in essence, a character in the story.

Exactly. Now, if Van Gogh was such a creator, then how might he gain immortality?

I didn't have to think long about that. By painting himself into his worlds.

As they say in clubs and halls and parlors across your great nation, 'Bingo.'

Okay, that made me laugh. While I digested this, I scanned the hillsides and mountainsides, looking for anything that obviously might be a hiding space, perhaps something far enough to be outside the search parameters of those looking for the girl. I continued widening my loop. A number of potential spots, upon closer inspection, proved to be tricks of light and shadow, nothing deep enough to be a cave system. Then again, the cave system was only a theory. For all I knew, the Red Rider had found an abandoned structure somewhere. Or was halfway around the world. No. He was presently working this side of the world. Perhaps he'd consumed all the viable magic in the old world. Perhaps the old world witches were being reborn *here* to escape him *there*. And the bastard was following the magic. That seemed plausible. Either way, he *had* been nearby, and I think he was *still* nearby. Somehow hiding from the angels, yet still needing to return to the third dimension to feed.

A profile of the man and his M.O. was emerging for me. Following the trail of magic, he snatched the most powerful of the children, disappearing from view from those searching in both the physical world and the angelic world, and at some point when he was ready... he feasted, which didn't end well for the victim.

It hadn't ended well for me, that's for sure.

Although I had no memory of it, I had a score to settle with this asshole. Yeah, it had long since gotten personal for me. A thought occurred to me.

Talos, you said your world exists in the fourth dimension, correct?

Correct.

Yet my physical three-dimensional body is presently in your four-dimensional world. How is that possible?

Oh, I've created a temporary inter-dimensional bubble, if you will. In essence, you still exist in the third dimension.

And what if that bubble should break?

Well, you might very well be trapped in the fourth dimension. But not to worry, Sam. I have control over the bubble, and it is a powerful intention.

But what if you should lose control of the bubble?

That won't happen.

But let's play 'what if.' Clearly, my body doesn't belong in the fourth dimension. What would happen to it?

Sam...

Just humor me.

Well, it might very well begin to disintegrate.

Yikes. Let's make a pact: never lose control of that inter-dimensional bubble thingy and I'll never wander out of it. Deal?

Deal.

A few beats of his mighty wings later, I asked if it was possible if the Red Rider used such an inter-dimensional bubble.

It's possible. The magic involved would be complex. I anchor the bubble from my dimension. He would have no anchor. In essence, he would have to fabricate his own.

Using magic?

Or convincing a being in the fifth dimension to anchor him, which I don't see as likely.

How so?

Fifth-dimensional beings are above even angels, Sam. These are holy, loving, devoted, spiritual beings. It would be a rarity indeed for such an entity to volunteer to anchor one such as the Red Rider.

So let's rule out a fifth-dimensional being anchoring him. But he could, theoretically, use magic to anchor himself?

He would have had to at least once temporarily found the fifth dimension on his own, through deep meditation and perhaps even astral projection.

The soul leaving the body?

Yes. Many humans have risen up through the dimensions on their own. Few can stay in the upper dimensions, but many have done it.

If the Red Rider were to find his way naturally to the fifth dimension, it's possible he could set an anchor?

Possible, but not likely. One cannot rise through the frequencies if one's intention is to exploit the frequencies. Had the intention been known, or felt by the universe, he would have just stayed in the third dimension, where impure inten-tions belong.

That feels like a jab at my dimension.

It is merely truth, Sam. The fourth dimension has its issues, too—we have, for instance, a humanoid uprising brewing in the caverns below—but such issues are not tainted by pure evil. Perhaps by misguided logic. However, such hostil-ities have been eradicated by the fifth dimension. The truth is, each dimension itself can be subdivided. In my case, my winged species lives in the upper fourth dimension. The humanoids in the lower fourth dimension. Your world is similar, with many more levels in the third dimension. Some of your humans are very high in the third dimension, and some of your humans are very low indeed.

But it is possible the Rider could have set an anchor for himself in the fifth dimension?

It would have taken a strong mind, Sam, to both fool himself and fool the universe; that is, to allow such an entity to rise through the frequencies. Then again, nothing is impossible. This universe allows for dreams and wishes and intentions to be fulfilled with enough belief. Had he wanted to set such an anchor in the fifth dimension, the universe would have provided a path for him. An unlikely path, but a path nonetheless. Whether or not he succeeded was up to him.

I think he succeeded.

If the angels have lost track of him, then I might have to agree. Mind you, had he been able to secure such an anchor, he would have been able to return to that spot time and time again via an inter-dimensional bubble.

But an anchor implies a connection, right? In theory, an anchor is attached to a line, which is itself attached to the boat.

Indeed, Sam. The Red Rider would have a life-line in this world.

I continued flying for another hour or so, and had just decided to call it a night when I felt an unusual pull in the direction of a distant rock outcropping that would have otherwise gone unnoticed. Okay, this is interesting.

That it is, Sam.

I banked to starboard and aimed in the direction of the rock cluster, as caves and more caves emerged from the shadow.

Very interesting indeed...

9.

Talos' wings caught the wind, slowing me to a landing atop a pile of rocks, where I summoned the single flame.

In an instant, the great dragon vanished, returning me to my naked human form. I paused and looked down at my body, amazed and delighted at the idea this mass of undead flesh I'd grown so fond of had just been to another world in the fourth dimension, a world I'd once lived on and mated on. I grinned at the strangeness of it all, then promptly refocused my thoughts. I had a child to find, and a killer to catch. I rummaged through my hide-a-bag for my clothing. Once dressed, I rolled up the hide-a-bag and shoved it into my back pocket. Handy for when one turns into a giant flying monster.

I stepped toward a promising cave opening that

looked more like a crease in the rock than anything. Then again, I didn't explore many caves. Maybe this was exactly what an opening should look like. Indeed, the subtle pull I felt from above came from in here. I took some worthless air and, with my heart actually picking up a beat or two, slipped through the rocky crease and into the cave, wondering what the hell I was about to get myself into...

***

Turned out, I'd entered a long, winding tunnel, which was undoubtedly pitch black for the average man. Luckily, I'm not the average man—or woman.

The light particles that only I—and others like me—could see, touched on everything, seemingly flowing through the rock themselves. Fang thought it was solar wind that emanated from the Sun. I didn't have much opinion on the matter. For now, it lit my way as I ventured deeper into the mountainside; that is, until I came to a crossroads.

The tunnel split to both the left and right. The subtle tug came from the right, and so I went that direction. As I did so... I heard it. The first of many rhythmic *whump, whump, whumps...*

Had I a heartbeat, I would have undoubtedly thought it was mine, somehow echoing in my ears. Perhaps I would have even convinced myself I was about to have a heart attack. But the bassy beating seemed to come from a direction ahead of me, even as it echoed through the rock enclosure.

In fact... I could feel the floor vibrating with each of the thumps. Not too long ago, I watched *Metropolis* with Kingsley, a silent movie that actually held my interest and moved me more than I thought possible. I imagined the beating I was hearing and feeling would have been similar to what the underground workers would have heard and felt being in such close proximity to the massive machines that ran the city above. An all-encompassing pulsating that vibrated everywhere.

The sound here wasn't so much loud as pervasive, reaching seemingly everywhere at once.

One thing I felt certain of... it was a heartbeat.

From whom or what, I hadn't a clue.

I crept deeper into the cave.

Deeper and deeper...

***

Small, bright lights scurried into dark corners that weren't really dark. The bright lights turned out to be bugs and spiders and even a rat or two, aglow to my eyes.

The cavern walls were dark basalt and seemed stable enough. I might be immortal, but I doubt I would survive a cave-in. I eased around a corner, then another, my hands gliding over rocky protrusions. All of it seemed natural, although I didn't know why. Just that nothing seemed chipped or chopped or blown up. No rock piles, either, and certainly no signs of human activity.

The beating grew louder. If I had to guess, I would have said someone was casually strumming a bass guitar, with the amp on high.

Whump, whump, whump...

Sometimes it would increase or decrease in tempo. I even found myself walking to the beat of the sound, two steps for every *whump*. Sometimes three and sometimes two, depending if the sound sped up slowed down. And yes... I could definitely feel it in the rock beneath me, seemingly rising up. But also in the walls too, as I slid my hand over the dusty outcroppings.

It was as if, yes... it was as if the mountain itself had a heartbeat.

Wow, okay... what was happening here?

I hadn't a clue, and so I continued on, aware that my inner alarm system barely made a blip. It sounded every now and then, but so faintly it verged on unnoticeable, especially with all the rhythmic beating going on around me. Meaning, whatever waited for me wasn't life threatening... at least not yet.

With each step, each turn, the tunnel grew warmer and the sound around me grew louder. I knew patrols of officers and park rangers, friends, family and community volunteers presently scoured the nearby hills and beaches for Annie. Except I was nowhere near their home. By my guess, I'd flown nearly forty miles away, deep into the rugged surrounding mountains where no ten-year-old girl would ever venture alone, and where no one would think to look for her, either.

That is, anyone not named Samantha Moon.

I felt Elizabeth rising to the surface, curious as hell about what I was getting myself into.

Not quite, child, came her hissing words. *I need to help keep you alive. Thisss thing that you are up against... it's no friend of ours.*

You are against the murder of children, magical or otherwise. Good to know you aren't a complete psychopath.

I am opposed to anything that might get you killed, Sssamantha Moon. As much as I despise your syrupy saccharine inner monologue, your desperate need for attention, and your vomitous attempt at romance with a hairy beast, I happen to still need you.

Always good to be needed.

For now, Sam Moon.

What does that...?

But I sensed what it meant. Once she got what she wanted, she had no more need for me. Once the seal had been broken, and once the dark masters flooded back in, there would be no more need for any of this back channel, possession shit.

That would mean...

Perhaps. Or perhaps not. Perhaps we can strike

a deal.

Bullshit, I thought. Once you bastards are in, you'll back out of your hosts, or explode out, or something. We will no longer be needed, and without your cursed dark magick, we will likely die... and instantly.

Now, Sssamantha. No need to get yourself worked up. Truth of the matter is, we don't know what will happen to our loving hosts.

Although we hadn't had too many conversations, I knew when Elizabeth was lying to me. Hell, I'd like to think I knew when anyone was lying to me. Sure, I had been told by the Creator himself that much of my ability resulted from my powerful soul being wholly contained in this physical body. But I also happened to know that my body was as good as dead, kept alive only by the dark masters' infernal formula of magicks, passed through the blood.

Yeah, as soon as that veil lifted, we were all dead. I was sure of it. Me, Kingsley, Fang... and any of the other "immortals" who roamed this planet. Granted, doing away with half of the ruthless vampires and werewolves wouldn't be a terrible thing. Except they would be replaced by the living, breathing dark masters themselves... which, I suspected, would be a much more terrible circumstance.

Now, now, now Sssamantha. You really can get yourself worked up. Obviously, that is only one such scenario. Another way to look at it is this: some of you wish for the sweet release of death, to be reunited with the Creator himself.

And leave the Earth to fend for itself.

Oh, we have many enemies. The war is not won, Sam. It will have only begun.

Not if I can help it, bitch. Back you go—

Please, Sssam. We got off on the wrong foot, as they say. I need to be present. I need to know what dark magicks you are up against and protect you. You are, after all, my greatest asset.

For now, I thought.

But she said nothing more, which was just as well. I told her she could tag along, but wanted her to keep quiet. She agreed by saying nothing at all. Smart woman.

Or whatever the hell she was.

Shortly after this fun exchange, I turned another corner, and found myself standing at the entrance to a large rock cavern... a cavern veritably pulsating with life. The walls, the ceiling, the floor... everything thrummed in time with the strange heartbeat.

I paused, swallowing, my mouth dry.

And then I spotted it sitting in the center of the room.

A wooden jewelry box. A throbbing, vibrating little wooden chest.

The beating came from within it.

"Sweet mama," I said for the second time that night, and stepped into the cavern.

10.

Of all the things I'd ever expected to find deep in a cave, a plain wooden box hadn't even made it on the list.

That it radiated a continuous heartbeat sound only added to the oddity of it. As I drew nearer, my hand extending to touch the lid, a tingle washed over me. Soft and prickly, as though I'd broken an electrified cobweb. I recognized the charge in the air from one other place—another time entirely. There had to be a ley line in this cave.

Oh, shit.

No wonder the Red Rider chose caves. Of course! Ley lines… that had to be where he got the power to shift his frequency from. I had no idea what this box was, nor why it emitted a beating heart sound. Still, I tentatively grabbed the lid and lifted it. Inside the shoebox-sized container, a miniature world of grass and sunlight existed. I'd have called it a diorama, but it felt far too real, as though I could somehow send myself into the box and go to another place entirely, a world that didn't look at all real, more like an impressionist painting.

I sighed out my nose and inhaled another needless gulp of air.

… and caught a scent. The unmistakable smell of a young human, along with the sourness of urine. Okay, what the hell is going on here?

Tammy, are you listening?

I stood there in silence for a few minutes waiting, calling out to my daughter a few more times.

Yeah, Mom. I'm here. Sorry. Anthony was being a butthead.

That probably involved bodily functions—I guessed farting—but that would be a bridge to cross for a later time.

Need your help, kiddo. Do you hear any other minds anywhere near mine?

A moment passed.

Umm. Not really.

Define 'really.' Does that mean there are, or there aren't?

Well… it's weird. There's something kinda farther away from me than where you are, but not too far. Like an area that's totally *calm and quiet. Almost like a hole in the universe.*

Hmm. Well, *that's* something.

I was half tempted to start calling out for Annie, but if that creature was here, I didn't want to give it any advanced warning. As powerful as it was, and with as much a habit as he had of disappearing into thin air, I figured my best chance would be an ambush strike.

As I maneuvered around the small rock pedestal holding the box, I drew the Devil Killer and headed for a passage that felt like the one Tammy thought about.

With each step I took down that passageway, the scent of child grew stronger. It unsettled me sometimes having such keen senses, but what unsettled me the most right then was the particular undertone of this smell. Mercifully, I did not smell fresh blood. I smelled stale saliva and bile. Also, a note of wet dirt and steel.

The cave curved to the right and went downhill for several minutes. Soon, a pale blue light shimmered up ahead. A whispery child's voice emitted soft grunts of exertion mingled with the delicate jingle of chain on rock. Oh, sweet mama. What the hell was this bastard doing to her?

I abandoned caution and ran as fast as I could move on foot. My vampiric reflexes did allow me to keep much quieter than a mortal, so perhaps the Red Rider might not notice me. Another bend came to the left. I whipped around it and crashed face first into a standing wall of blue light.

Ouch.

What on Earth... this bastard had a force field?

Patterns drifted around in concentric circles within the transparent barrier. Beyond lay a more featureless brownish cave with a sharp rightward bend not far from where I found myself stuck. I hated to think it, but this magical wall with all the dancing marks inside it resembled something out of *Doctor Strange.* That gave me an idea.

Tammy? Can you share what I'm seeing here with Allison? How do I get past this?

"Hello?" asked a weak child's voice. "Is someone there?" Chain clinked. "Help! Please!"

Grr. I balled my hands in fists, simultaneously wanting to comfort her and terrified the Red Rider would merely disappear again if I gave myself away. Screw it. I could apologize later for scaring her. That sounded a lot easier than trying to *find* her again. I may not get the chance to.

Allison says it's a magical barrier.

I blinked. Thank you, Captain Obvious.

She said don't be mean. She's contacting her ghost friend.

Millie?

Yes, her.

I knew Allison had recently had the mother of all adventures, including tangling with an Aztec god and watching her cruise ship sink to the bottom of the ocean. She still didn't want to talk about it, which was fine with me. But I do know she had thought she had lost Millie forever, thinking her witchy ghost friend was bound in a bottle of dirt (a long story that I still wasn't entirely privy to), but that had proven not to be the case. Turned out, a ghost couldn't be contained... like ever.

Hold on, Mom. She's still talking to Millie the ghost, and, hey, I could tell you everything that went down with her and the god thing.

I know you can, baby. But I'll let Allison come around.

I waited a few agonizing seconds, during which the distant child lapsed into weak sobs, begging no one in particular to 'please let me out of here.'

My blood nearly boiled.

Okay, Mom. Whoa. Calm down. I've never seen you that pissed off... wait. Yeah, I have. When you-know-who tricked me.

I folded my arms.

Yeah. Messing with you or Anthony is the best way to make me irrationally angry. This comes close. Look. How do I get past this thing?

Okay... Allison said you'd need to start raising a barrier with an opposing energy in the same space as this one and the two energies would counteract each other—if you're stronger or as strong as the one that's there.

Need I remind you that I am not a witch?

You should have been, rasped Elizabeth.

"And whose fault is that?" I grumbled.

"Hello?" whispered Annie—at least I felt certain I'd found her. The odds of me stumbling on another child in this cave were pretty damn low.

Dammit. "Shh," I whispered. "Please stay quiet. I'm here to help."

Chain rattled as the girl whispered, "I wanna go home. Please help!"

"Yeah. That's the plan. Please stay quiet, sweetie."

"The monster's not here. He's sleeping."

"Sleeping?"

"Yeah," whispered Annie. "Like a balloon with no air in it."

Whoa, said Tammy in my head. *I don't even want to know what that means. Anyway, Allison says you're not a witch but you are a vampire with an angel sword.*

How is that supposed to help me deal with magic?

Allie says touch the earth with bare skin, stick the sword against the barrier like you're trying to kill it, and want with all your strength to call energy up from the earth to reabsorb the magic.

We're right back to the 'me not being a witch' thing.

Trust her. She's going to send energy to you.

I sighed, crouched, and pressed my left hand to the ground. With my right, I stabbed the point of the Devil Killer into the transparent blue wall. It resisted, but I pushed as hard as I could—almost shoving myself over backward due to the ungainly squat. Oh, screw it. Guess there's a reason witches and druids always went barefoot—or bare-assed like my brother Clayton. Though, he had no inclination toward witchcraft. Total hippie.

After removing a shoe, I planted one bare foot on the ground and took a balanced stance, the Devil Killer held in two hands, point at the center of the barrier. With all the strength I could summon, I pushed.

Though she didn't send words, I knew Tammy had passed along my readiness to Allison. I concentrated as much as I could on wanting that barrier out of my way, on wanting Annie to be safe.

And wanting the Red Rider to die a thousand times over for the horrors he'd committed on the innocent.

"Are you still there?" whispered Annie. "Please… I'm *so* hungry."

Can. Not. Let. My. Concentration. Break.

I pushed.

I growled.

I snarled even.

Perhaps a bit of drooling occurred.

Okay, channeling Kingsley here isn't helping.

Tingles of energy came up from the ground into my foot, up my leg, and flooded my body with a warm sensation a bit less than painful—like I'd touched a live electrical wire without *that* much current in it.

Ugh, this isn't working.

Seconds later, the energy intensified to painful.

What had been a little sharper than tickling everywhere became a swarm of biting, stinging insects. As my desire to get to this girl peaked, the air around me crackled and shimmered, and the barrier imploded with a soft *whump.*

All the force I'd been pushing against it with launched me three steps forward, only my supernatural reflexes stopped me from doing a faceplant that would've gotten a perfect ten at the Derp Games. In my haste to get to this child, I completely forgot my abandoned shoe and rushed around the corner to the end of the tunnel, where it connected to a roundish chamber of brown stone.

Annie rested on the ground at the middle of the bowl-shaped chamber floor, wearing the partially shredded remains of a pretty peach-colored dress, a fair amount of dirt, and no shoes. Her long, blonde hair had become a wild tear-soaked tangle. The Red Rider had chained her spread eagled to iron stakes pounded into the earth like a frog from biology class pinned to the tray for dissection. I hated my brain for going there. Annie and that frog faced a similar fate, only the scientists had been kind enough to euthanize the frog before they started cutting it open. Red smears of strange ritualistic squiggles covered her arms and shoulders. Similar red marks painted her face, arms and legs, right to the tips of her toes.

I nearly fainted at the sight of all that red, until I caught a whiff of plant matter. Paint or ink of some kind. Holy shit. Whew. *Not* blood. He hasn't started cutting her yet. I practically melted with relief. Annie raised her head to stare at me, her blue eyes wide with dread, and futilely struggled at the chains with almost no strength left in her limbs. My heart broke at the same time it exploded with rage. That little girl could barely move—and she'd been like that for days, no doubt. She'd been fighting so hard her wrists were covered in bruises. That sight set off an explosion of rage inside me. Elizabeth writhed at the back of my mind, adoring my fury. Despite it probably being dangerous to do anything that woman enjoyed, seeing Annie in such a state so infuriated me that I didn't really care that much.

Had the Red Rider done this to Daisy... who had also been me in another life? And to his other victims? Part of me was glad memories didn't carry over from past reincarnations.

A lump of... fabric and leather sat on the floor at the right side of the chamber, like a renaissance festival wizard had dropped his costume to go skinny dipping—or an inflatable inquisitor lost all his air. I crept toward Annie, sword raised as I scanned around for any sign of the Red Rider. It would, of course, be just like that fiend to leave the child out there like bait and ambush me from a blind angle.

Again, Annie struggled, fighting hard to move, to sit up, to do anything to get to me. The rustle of chains and her rapid, desperate breaths seemed deafening. Her terrified expression left me little doubt she knew exactly—well maybe not *exactly*—what this thing meant to do to her, but I was pretty sure she expected to die here.

Tammy, miles away in the hotel, burst into tears. *Oh, my God, Mom. Get her out of there!*

Working on it, I thought back to her. Don't want to be jumped from behind. This looks like a trap. I stepped closer and whispered, "Hang on, Annie. I'm here to help."

For an instant, the girl stared at me like *I* was the horrible monster she couldn't get away from, and fought her bonds harder, gasping and whimpering.

"Y-you're n-not alive. Y-you're…"

"Complicated." I took a knee beside her and put on my most comforting, motherly smile while pulling her hair away from her eyes. "Annie, please know that I would never hurt you."

She gulped. Dried saliva coated her cheeks and chin. The poor kid didn't look like she'd had anything to eat or much at all to drink in days. The wretched reek of urine fouled the air. Since he hadn't given her any food or water, the filth didn't amount to that much. Ugh. Still, she'd been like this for about a week, never let out.

My jaw dropped open in pure horror, then clenched in rage. Such abject cruelty. "You… he's…"

"Starving me," said Annie, oddly calm. "He's

going to kill me. But he told me he won't do it until I'm so weak I can barely talk."

If he killsss her now, Sssamantha, he will merely end her life. He must weaken the poor innocent, helpless child to steal her magic. As he has done with all his victimsss. Even your prior incarnation. Starved to delirium then devoured alive. It is not an easy death. Perhaps the only fate worse would be scaphism. Wonderfully gruesome method of execution, that. I could explain it to you sometime if you're curious.

Hard Pass.

Touché, said Elizabeth with a hint of a smile in her tone.

I felt Tammy cringe. *Mom. That bitch inside you is such a bitch.*

Since I did *not* like the look of the arcane markings painted all over the girl, I smeared the hell out of them as best I could with my sleeve. I did remember hearing Allison once say that this sort of thing required a lot of precision, so ruining it was easy.

"Please let me out. I don't know where the key is. I'm *so* scared." She squirmed. "Maybe it's over there with his stuff."

"What happened to him?"

"I don't know. When he finished painting on me, he walked over there and just… melted."

A fading spark in Annie's eyes brightened the instant I smeared the markings on her forehead. I'm not entirely sure what I did, but cleaning her up any more is going to require water and soap—and getting her the hell out of this cave is more important. I grabbed the manacle around her tiny wrist in both hands, and pulled at it until the lock snapped open. Annie cradled her arm to her chest, whimpering in pain.

I grabbed the manacle on her left wrist, and snarled, perhaps a bit more deeply than a human ought to be able to.

"Umm," whispered Annie.

"Sorry. Don't be scared. I'm not going to hurt you. Almost there." I grunted, and snapped the manacle open.

"Look out!" shouted Annie. She flung herself up to sit and grabbed me, shaking in fear. "He's back!"

I whirled to peer over my shoulder. The formerly deflated pile of regalia nearly stood to its full height, rising only an inch or two more after I looked at it.

The Red Rider had returned—and he didn't look happy to see me.

11.

Annie clung to me, trembling. The chains still attached to her ankles rattled.

A momentary spike of anticipation wafted from Elizabeth, like a child seeing presents under the Christmas tree. Of course, she adored violence. I had a good feeling I was about to experience quite a bit of it. Either that, or she expected this thing would be so powerful I'd have to ask her for help and she'd finally break out of the mind vault.

The scariest of notions crossed my thoughts. To save myself, I'd never let her out. To protect this innocent child? If it came down to that, I…

My thoughts cut off when I made eye contact with pure evil.

No longer deflated, the tainted inquisitor stood there as solid and real as anything. A dark crimson hooded cloak concealed his face, draped over ancient leather armor with numerous belts and sashes holding pouches, knives, and traveling gear. The dude looked like he stepped straight out of five centuries ago. He lifted his head enough that the hood revealed eyes of infinite darkness. Not merely black, they drank in light, holes in the fabric of reality itself. A red sash covered the lower half of the Red Rider's face. He had a powerful build like a Roman centurion, short hair, and a few scars nicked the bridge of his nose and forehead. One red mark looked as though he'd come close to losing an eye.

Annie emitted a tiny grunt, pulling at the chain connecting her right ankle to a stake. "Please don't let him get me."

Well, at least he won't run off with her, Sssamantha. She's still tethered to the ground.

Grr. Not funny.

Tammy's fear blew across my mind. Anthony and Allison were in the midst of freaking out about me running off on my own and here this monster was. Kingsley—according to Tammy's thoughts—was already on the way to me, guided by my daughter's general sense of where my thoughts came from.

They'd never get here in time.

The Red Rider drew a gladius from his belt.

I stepped in front of Annie, raising the Devil Killer. "I'm afraid I have to revoke your witch hunting permit. This one's not big enough. Should'a thrown her back in."

"I'm not a trout!" shouted Annie.

Ooh. I liked this kid.

"And fishing is mean. They deserve to live, too."

Without a word—or a noticeable change in facial expression—the abomination rushed at me. I threw all the mojo I could into strength, speed, and agility, swinging my sword at his gladius like I wanted to cut it in half. The Red Rider slowed down, nearly halting like a mannequin. My blade rang off his with a bell-like *clang* of steel, knocking him into a sideways stumble.

Whoa. I was not expecting that. This horrible monster was no faster or stronger than a mortal human? But then again, how fearsome did one have to be to terrorize teenage witches, or in this case, a ten-year-old?

Snarling, I leapt after him, committing myself wholly into a two-handed swing I hoped would cut him clean in half through the chest. He got his left arm up in time, the Devil Killer striking a Frisbee-sized shield strapped to his forearm with a wooden *thunk*. My blade left a searing burn line on the aged buckler amid a faint shower of sparks. The Red Rider flew most of the way across the cave, landed on his back, and rolled to his feet.

If I caught him off guard, worried him, or otherwise triggered any sort of emotion in him, it didn't show in his eyes at all.

Annie struggled to stand, but the stakes kept her feet too far apart, so she gave up and fell back on her rear end.

Light appeared at the Red Rider's gloved hands and washed over him.

"Careful!" rasped Annie. "He's made himself stronger!"

Anthony says he just 'buffed himself.'

Not now, Tammy. I'm not sure I want to know about your brother 'buffing himself.'

Eww, Mom. Really? It's from video games. He's talking about that thing you're fighting... like he did magic or something to make himself more powerful.

The Red Rider blurred into a streak, coming straight at me. I barely managed to get the Devil Killer up. That time when our blades crossed, *my* ass went flying. I bounced off the cave wall and landed flat on my chest.

"Oof." I growled. "Okay, bastard. It's gonna be like that, huh? Let's dance."

He again blurred, appearing over me in an instant, poised to spear me in the heart through my back... not that it would've done much but hurt.

I think.

A blast of yellowish light flew from Annie's hand, striking the Rider in the head with the force of a punch. Hood smoking, he staggered away from me. Annie, still sitting on the floor with her legs chained to stakes, gestured again, and another glowing projectile sailed from her hand and hit him in the shoulder.

Tammy tried—and failed—not to let her thoughts leak that Allison doubted I would survive taking on the Red Rider alone. Hey, I'm not technically alone. Annie's helping. And I kinda sorta had Elizabeth on my side, too, I think. It was, after all, in the bitch's best interest to keep me alive.

I sprang upright and called on my powers as if I faced the Devil all over again. Underestimating this creature would only get me killed. My vampire reflexes sped me up, dragging time into a blurry, sluggish mess. My body hung in mid leap, flying toward the Red Rider who circled to the side in a tactical retreat, giving ground. Despite the relative sluggishness of my 'glide,' we swung back and forth at each other while slow-motion magical projectiles drifted by no faster than leaves gliding on a breeze. In reality, my leap took barely two seconds, and in that time our swords clashed a dozen times. His centuries of experience with a blade compensated for my advantage in speed. We stalemated, sparks flying as our weapons crossed again and again.

The instant my toes touched the cave floor, one of Annie's magic bolts caught him in the face, incinerating the red sash over his mouth and nose, revealing the lower half of his face to be little more than skull. Though it didn't seem to hurt him much more than a punch, Annie's attack shoved his head to the left.

I capitalized on the distraction, swinging at his neck like I wanted a home run.

The Red Rider recovered, but not fully in time to stop me. His gladius scraped down the edge of my descending sword, pushing my aim point to the right. The Devil Killer hacked several inches into his shoulder. Smoke and flames burst from the cut, gathering in a whorl around my hands as though the weapon had ignited.

For the first time, the Red Rider's eyes gave away a trace of emotion—he looked concerned as he stumbled away from me, smoke peeling from the gash. Black blood rolled down his leather chestplate and sizzled on the front end of my blade.

"She's an innocent child!" I shouted, raising the sword. "How dare you!"

On wings of rage, I charged after him. He leapt to the side, narrowly ducking my telegraphed attack. Again, I slashed, but he backpedaled after parrying, spinning about and raising a small pistol crossbow which had been somewhere under that massive cloak.

But he didn't point it at me.

He fired the quarrel at Annie. In my accelerated reflex state, the projectile appeared to glide forward like a lazy bird. Without hesitation, I twisted after it, jumping to grab the quarrel out of the air. Only when the Red Rider darted around me did I realize the shot had been intended as a diversion. However, he hadn't aimed to miss her.

Clutching the wound in his shoulder, the Red Rider sprinted into the passage I'd taken into this chamber, two sluggish magical bolts from Annie chasing him. The crossbow quarrel had surprising strength, pulling me a step or two forward. Forced to choose between stepping on Annie or tripping over the chain, I took the faceplant.

That said, I faceplanted like an Olympic gymnast and wound up back on my feet in less than a second. Pissed, I raced after the fleeing red cloak. Cave blurred by, the constant *thump, thump, thump,* of that weird box growing louder. I dashed into the first chamber the same instant the Red Rider opened the lid on the little shoebox. As fast as I could push myself to move, I charged, but my swing passed through a vanishing red haze.

The Red Rider flowed into the shoebox with no more solidity than a cloud of crimson smoke.

What the... what the?

Elizabeth emitted a sudden blast of rage which I echoed. For once, we were in complete accord.

I may have screamed several words that I probably shouldn't have screamed in earshot of a ten-year-old.

The interior of the shoebox still looked like an impressionist painting, but a tiny red figure ran off across the field. I was *so* damn tempted to jump in after him and end this, but... I couldn't leave Annie shackled to stakes. That poor girl had already been stuck here so long without food and water that she was going to need to be hospitalized. And that business about disintegrating in other dimensions also held me back. I'm not attuned to any higher frequencies, so if I wound up lost in there, I could very well destroy myself roaming around.

That thought appeared to quell Elizabeth's rage as well. Or at least stoppered it in a bottle for now.

I sprinted back to the other chamber where Annie had resumed her tug-of-war with the remaining stakes.

"Help!" She paused in her futile effort to break the manacle off her right ankle. "Wow. How did you break these?"

The sight of a child in such a state broke my heart all over again. "It's complicated. Come on. Let's get you home."

She leaned back and waited patiently while I grabbed and snapped the last two manacles off her legs. Once I freed her, she struggled to her feet, but whimpered in pain and started to collapse. I caught and cradled her tight.

Annie snuggled to me, barely enough strength in her arms to hold on. "Thank you. I thought I was going to die."

Talk about messed up. She's a ten-year-old who'd been kidnapped and left helpless in a cave for a week… and I'm the one who burst into tears.

12.

"Umm," said Annie.

"What's wrong?" I asked, sliding the Devil Killer back into its magical sheath.

She emitted a nervous laugh. "I've never had my neck so close to a vampire's mouth before."

I relaxed my embrace and looked into her eyes. "Do you believe in reincarnation?"

"Yes. The fairies told me about it once."

"The *thing* that attacked you also kidnapped one of my past selves a long time ago. My father… well, one-time father from long ago, wasn't able to fight him. But he was only a mortal. So, yeah, I'm not like other vampires."

Nausea rolled over my brain from Elizabeth. *So insufferable. She's merely a child. So what if she dies? There are millions more. But, at least this one is special. She's a witch like I was, and you can't be. That's worth at least thirty normal ones.*

Grr. Before I could slam the door on Elizabeth, she withdrew into the mental box of her own accord.

"Thank you for saving me," rasped Annie. "I thought I was gonna die. Like, for reals."

I squeezed her. "You're safe now."

Eyes closed, I concentrated on the dancing flame and pictured the field near the eucalyptus tree, near enough to her house to walk back and far enough away that no one would likely see us appear out of thin air.

My attempt to teleport ended with a sensation like I'd walked into a wall of gelatin. Damn. This cave must be warded… or the ley lines are messing with me. Hopefully, it's only this chamber. Or maybe it's that heart box. Either way… time to walk a little. I headed out, carrying Annie. After being staked down in an X for days, I'm sure her muscles were too sore for much of anything.

"He told me he was gonna starve me. Said I was a witch and I deserved to die for it."

"That *creature* is evil. He was lying. You do not deserve to die. He only wants to steal your power for himself."

"Was he really gonna kill me?"

I bit my lip, then sighed. No point BS-ing the kid. "Yes. But, you're safe now."

"He ruined my dress," said Annie in a tired,

annoyed tone. "To put the bad magic on me."

A glimmer appeared to my left. I turned toward it and, for an instant, locked stares with a woman I figured to be the girl's guardian angel. A flicker of silver light glinted in her eyes, and a rush of insight hit me. The Red Rider had painted a ritual spell on Annie's body that trapped her power inside her, preventing her from using any magic, talking to the Earth, and even blocking her from the guardian angel's sight.

I half wanted to question how the Red Rider managed to take Annie away from her in the first place, but I didn't think this poor kid got stuck with an idiot of a guardian angel like I had. No, she hadn't done anything on purpose here. Somehow, the Red Rider had a way around guardians. Lucky for me, I no longer relied on one. Neither did Anthony. And Tammy's got two: her actual angel, and Anthony... and well, me. I had wings, so I guess I counted a little more than metaphorically as an angel.

In the back of my mind, I experienced a vague notion of Tammy and Allison jumping around hugging each other in joy that I'd rescued the girl. As soon as I walked past the point where the magical barrier had been, the dancing flame brightened. Annie didn't react to the thumping box in the next chamber beyond shivering at the eerie heartbeat noise. I stooped to collect my shoe and put it back on. Then, holding her tight, I called out to the flame. In seconds, the creepy-ass heartbeat gave way to the idle chirping of birds and the gentle rustle of wind in the leaves.

"Whoa," whispered Annie. "That was awesome… we teleported! How did you do that?"

"Special magic." I opened my eyes and gazed around at the grove near her house, specifically, the enormous old tree.

No sense leaving this kid with nightmares of being tied to stakes in a cave for a week, alone in the dark while slowly starving to near-death. Thank God that she had no idea what the Red Rider would really have done to her.

I held her out far enough to again look into her eyes. Erasing that memory would only take a moment or four.

"Please don't." Annie blinked, looking away. "I know you're trying to make me forget. Please let me remember so I can protect myself."

Holy crap. This kid just resisted my mental influence. Though, I hadn't really pushed hard at all. "Umm. Are you sure about that? What you went through… you're going to have nightmares."

Annie shivered. "Maybe. But I'm a witch. My life's gonna be full of strange, weird stuff like this. I would like to remember. I'm okay. I promise not to spend the next five years hiding under my bed."

I set her on her feet and took a knee, brushing her matted hair off her face. "You are incredibly brave for a kid. For anyone, actually."

She smiled. "What's your name?"

"Samantha Moon."

"That's pretty." Annie managed a smile.

A swarm of fairy lights welled out of the branches and surrounded us in a whirlwind of color. Three light balls gathered around the child's chest, lifting the shredded flaps of her dress back to her neck and… mending it. Others brightened, gliding close to her body. The visible effects of not eating for a week faded. Annie appeared to bask in the healing touch of their magic, and after a moment, she merely looked dirty and disheveled, no longer in need of immediate hospitalization. Okay, wow.

She laughed and held her arms out, allowing the fairies to land on her. I'm sure she saw them as little people, while to me they remained light dots. With her safe again, I couldn't help but feel somehow jealous. Not toxically jealous though. I didn't resent her for what she had, more that I felt an inexplicable sense of loss for my magic having been taken from me.

It didn't make any sense considering I'd never thought twice about it until this whole Red Rider thing started. It almost made me suspect some external force worked on my mind, dredging at these feelings. Missing my connection with the fairies or the Earth, being blocked out of Allison's thoughts or the trifecta. I felt like a kid whose parents forced her to move to a new city for a year, then returned home only to find my two best friends had replaced me with some other kid and no longer wanted me around. That trifecta should've been *my* destiny this life.

Ugh. Now I knew something was wrong with me. I shouldn't be getting clingy and possessive over Allison, her witches, or any of that stuff. It wasn't who I am.

Ahh yes, but it is who you should have been, Sssamantha. Things were *stolen from you. It is quite normal to mourn such a loss, even desire that which was taken from you. What harm can there be in you simply wanting it? People want things they cannot have all the time. Look at me. It isss a healthy part of being human.* She paused, then followed with an insincere, *Oops.*

I shook my head. I'm still human. Just not mortal.

No, Sssmantha Moon. You are very far from being human. Very far indeed.

Okay, that was weird.

Meanwhile, Annie smiled seemingly everywhere at once. "Thank you!" she chirped at the fairies. "Yes. She found me." Her expression drooped to a worried stare. "No. He got away."

The unmistakable sense that all the light balls turned to look at me came on.

"Oh, this isn't over. Not by a long shot." I shook my head. "I couldn't leave her there like that while I chased that thing around."

A wave of contentment—or at least momentary

satisfaction—wafted from the cloud of dancing lights. They massed around Annie for a moment or two more, then returned to the branches of the great tree except for one brilliant lavender light ball that remained on her shoulder.

Annie looked up at me without any trace of her former hesitation or fear of my vampiric nature. "Thank you for saving me. My friends are really happy I'm okay." She bowed her head, a curtain of blonde falling over her face. Whoa—when did her hair become clean and funk-free? "They didn't think they'd ever see me again. I should go home. My parents are really upset."

"Yes. They have been so worried for you, but they're going to be thrilled."

Elizabeth saturated my head with a pervasive sense of 'ugh' at the imminent approach of hugging, crying, squeezing and emotional outpouring. Evidently not wanting to be part of that, she self-exiled into her mental prison, slammed the sewer cover, and put the boulder on the lid herself.

"Miss Moon?" whispered Annie.

"It's all right if you want to call me Samantha. Both of our lives have been touched by that abomination." I silently thanked nothing in particular that I didn't remember it.

She clasped my hand. "Is that monster going to come after me again?"

I narrowed my eyes at the trees. "Not if I have anything to say about it."

Annie continued staring at me, worried.

"Hey, remember... he ran away from me. He's scared."

She ground her toe into the dirt. "Not as scared as I was."

"You were way braver than I would've been... throwing spells at him like that."

"When you broke the markings, I got my magic back." She wiped at her arms.

"Oh, crap. That's going to be difficult to explain."

Annie froze and looked up. "Huh?"

"Where I found you and how I freed you. Your parents didn't seem entirely... cool with the whole magic and fairies thing."

She shrugged. "It doesn't freak them out too much anymore, but me being kidnapped and almost killed might be too much for them."

"It's going to mess with the police."

"Seriously? They called the police?"

I patted her on the head. "Hon, their child was missing and they had no idea *what* took you. Of course they called the police."

"Is lying to the police bad?"

"Yes. But. Lying to the police to protect them isn't bad."

"Protect them from what?"

I bit my lip. Oh, a life of hard drinking, divorce, maybe padded cells and straitjackets. No way was I going to say that to a kid though, so instead, I said,

"Magic stuff they can't understand and can't do anything about. They'll be much happier not knowing the truth. So yes, we do need to lie to them a little. I'm going to make them believe that you were kidnapped by a normal person." I tapped a finger to my chin. "Some crazy old woodland hermit who saw you out here and mistook you for his daughter."

Annie held up her arms. "My wrists are cut and bleeding from the chain—" She blinked in awe at her arms, still bloody, but no longer cut. They were, in fact, healed. A flash of realization hit her and she spun to grin at the tree. "Thank you!"

The eucalyptus gave off a pulse of happiness.

She said, "There's a stream right over there. Let me wash this stuff off. It's still icky." Annie started walking, but the lavender light ball on her shoulder took flight, orbiting her in a rapid spiral.

Every bit of paint—and the dried blood on her arms—peeled away and fell to the grass.

"Oh, wow." She gently grasped the fairy and hugged… her? "Thank you!"

I smiled at the spectacle, then scooped Annie up and walked toward the house.

"Why are you carrying me?"

"You spent a week unable to move. Your arms and legs must be sore. Besides, you don't have any shoes on."

"I only wear shoes to school and stuff. Not around home. And I'm not sore."

"Okay, I'm carrying you because I was so desperate to find you before he hurt you that I'm a giant child who needs to hug a doll right now."

She laughed for a moment, then clung, shivering.

"You sure you don't want me to make you forget that?" I asked.

Annie kept quiet, likely considering. "Nah. I'll be okay. Your skin is cold."

"I know."

"Are you dead?"

"Kinda."

"You are a good vampire."

"I try to be. Sometimes I fail."

"Will I see you again?"

I smiled. "Of that, I have no doubt."

"You talk funny."

"I know. Adults are weird."

The lavender light ball glided up to my shoulder. It appeared about ready to alight, but decided against it and glided back around to settle on Annie's chest, where parts of her torn dress had been made whole again. I refused to think about the Red Rider attacking this innocent child with all his torturer's tools. There wouldn't have been much left of the dress—or of Annie—when he finished.

Before I grew too angry to think, I blocked those thoughts for now. I'd tap that anger when I found the Red Rider.

On the way back to the house, Annie and I

concocted a story for the cops. She'd been out playing in the grove as she always did when a man ran by and grabbed her. Clearly out of his mind, he believed she was his kid who had been kidnapped and dragged her away to a cave. Other than keeping her in a locked room, he'd been reasonably nice to her. I invented a fictitious image of a nonexistent crazy hermit and showed it to her mentally... just in case one of the cops came back to talk to her later.

We planned to give the parents the real story. If they couldn't cope with the bizarre truth, they'd also believe the fake crazy man grabbed her. I questioned my judgment allowing a ten-year-old child to keep her memories of an ordeal like that, but admittedly, I had the sense this girl *could* handle it. Tossing magical bolts like that at ten, this kid's going to be a witchy prodigy.

A few minutes later, I carried Annie out of the trees into the yard behind her house and proceeded around to the front door. Since she lay sideways across my arms, she stretched out a leg and pushed the doorbell with her big toe.

Gene answered. And promptly shouted for his wife. Tears literally sprang from his eyes.

"Daddy!" wailed Annie, finally sounding like a child who'd just been through hell.

I handed her over and she clamped onto him, then burst into sobs. As calm as she'd been the whole time, I suspected she laid it on thick, but no... as far as I could read from her, she'd willfully kept her composure until that moment. Being home, seeing her parents, she lowered her defenses and let all her terror out.

Rita ran over and joined the hug, also bursting into tears.

A plainclothes detective I didn't recognize and two FBI agents got up from the sofa and walked over, their expressions conveying astounded relief. For the next hour and change, we sat in their living room while Annie and I related the concocted story of her kidnapping. Her parents shared a loveseat with the kid in their lap. Annie clung, trembled, and couldn't stop crying. Even a precociously mature ten-year-old couldn't really handle knowing the man—*thing*—that abducted her had every intention to kill her.

So, yeah, I decided to play with her memory just a little bit since I couldn't stand seeing her that terrified. One minor change: the Red Rider intended to drain all her magic and leave her a normal non-magical kid. Which is a three-quarter truth. I didn't specify a normal *living* kid. With that edit, she regained most of her composure and scaled back from total freak-out to 'highly upset.'

Not quite ten minutes into the interview, the doorbell rang again. Tammy, Anthony, and Allison joined us. I couldn't help myself and squeezed both my kids tight the whole time. Tammy fidgeted, embarrassed at me being all clingy with her in front of strangers, but she knew full well what I saw in that cave and what my mind tortured me with knowing would've happened to Annie… so she tolerated being used as a plushie. Of course, that made me think back to when she'd been four years old, I'd been a mortal, and shot in the line of duty at HUD. Not knowing exactly what was wrong with Mommy, my daughter tried to make me feel better by sitting close and hugging me. Tammy—in the here and now—blushed scarlet at my remembering that, and a miracle occurred: she dropped the teen attitude for a little while and clung to me the same way she did back then.

I couldn't help but notice the 'I wish we were all still normal' stare in her eyes. It became unclear at that point who consoled who. I couldn't forget that my daughter's gift was driving her ever so slowly—okay, not that slowly—insane. As soon as I dealt with the Red Rider, I would scour every mystical library in the world hunting for a way to help her control her rampant telepathy.

With a little mental nudge from yours truly, the detective and the FBI agents held no suspicions about the story, accepting the crazy hermit fabrication as absolute fact. I do feel somewhat guilty that they're going to waste resources combing an area of empty forest about sixty miles north of here… but that's better than Annie winding up involuntarily committed for mental evaluation.

The normal authorities expressed their happiness that Annie had been found alive, and left.

Within minutes of their departure, Kingsley arrived. He'd had to run all the way back from wherever he'd gone off in search of me. He gave me a 'we'll talk later' look that suggested he intended to 'scold' me for charging off alone.

With the normal authorities gone, I gingerly explained to the parents what really happened. I didn't see any need to torture them with the gruesome details of what he intended to do to her beyond stealing her magic. I telepathically told Rita and Gene that he would have undoubtedly killed her, while simultaneously explaining that Annie remained unaware that she would've died, merely been rendered magicless. I also prompted the parents with the idea that Annie's magic was the best possible way to protect her, so they should accept her for who she was and what she can do.

As easy a time as I had doing that, I'm sure the parents had largely made deals with the powers that be that they'd accept the weird stuff if only they could have her back alive.

And hey, for all I know, I am merely a cog in the machinery of the Universe as it functioned to make that deal with them.

Either way, Annie's alive. She escaped the fate that befell my former self. I spared Gene the torment that my once-father suffered.

I could live with that.

You're dead, Sssam.

Yeah. Yeah. Technicalities.

13.

Elizabeth retreated again when I went to leave and Annie's parents hugged and sobbed all over me for a good ten minutes.

"I don't know where you came from or why you got involved, but *thank you!*" Gene shook my hand so hard I expected it to come off in his grip. "This is cliché as hell, but there's nothing we can ever do that will repay you for this."

I smiled. "Believe your daughter. Embrace her gift. Be the best parents you can be and I'll call it even."

Rita wiped tears and hugged me again. "You're an angel!"

"I only play one on TV."

Anthony snickered.

"What?" I glanced at him. "Really, I'm just

kinda winging it here."

Tammy groaned.

Allison shook her head at me.

"All right. I really should go get started on finding that thing." By now, everyone present knew what that "thing" was.

"Wait!" yelled Annie. She let go of her parents and zipped over to stand in front of me.

The little lavender light ball on her shoulder, quite well hidden amid her hair, appeared to be whispering in her ear.

Annie reached both hands up. "Take my hands."

I did.

She closed her eyes.

A moment later, her hair fluttered on a breeze that didn't exist. Green and yellow light comets emerged from thin air around her, orbiting us both. They whirled faster and faster until they smeared into rings. Her parents watched this spectacle with raised eyebrows and no color in their cheeks. Kingsley quirked one eyebrow. Allison had a face on like a professor watching one of their students figure something out on their own. My son's expression more or less gave off a 'that's pretty cool' vibe, while Tammy had resumed the teen surly stare at nothing in particular.

I suspected she actually made that face while trying to concentrate on *not* hearing all the thoughts going on around her. Her non-reaction to that idea in my head kinda proved it.

The orbiting lights collapsed into me, settling as a brief warmth in my gut before fading away.

"There," said Annie. "We both touched that monster. Maple told me you kinda have a way to find him. I just tried to make it stronger."

"True. I have a link to him... somehow. Maple?"

Annie beamed. "The fairy! Her name isn't really Maple, but I call her that 'cause her real name is too hard to say."

Hmm. I didn't sense anything had changed. Still, if a kid gives you artwork they made, no matter how unrecognizable it is, you act like they handed you a Picasso. Even though her spell didn't seem to have any effect, I decided not to question it. "Awesome. Thank you!"

She leapt into a hug, squeezing me. "Thank you so much for saving me."

"I'm just glad I was able to find you."

"Miss Moon..." Little Annie leaned back enough to stare into my eyes. "You messed with my head, didn't you? I know you did something but I can't tell what."

"I only made a minor change so you could handle it all better. Just made things a little less scary. I didn't change anything you lived through or saw."

"Okay. That's cool. Maple says whatever you did was good for me, so I won't be upset."

Tammy rolled her eyes. *Thank God she's not*

mad at you, ma. It's not like you saved her ass or anything.

Go back deeper, I thought, and you'll see we had an agreement. I kinda broke the agreement.

Hard pass. I get enough information coming at me without having to go looking for more.

Fine. Then ease back on the attitude, young lady.

Her eyes started up again, but stopped in mid-roll—which looked like it might have hurt.

She laughed. *You're such a dork, Mom.*

I grinned, and we proceeded through the emotional farewell process. Allison left her card in case Annie had any questions about witchy stuff. No sooner did we all climb into the Momvan than Kingsley ranted a little bit about my going off alone. He didn't 'yell at me,' just aired how frustrated he was that he couldn't help.

"You're right," I said. "I'm sorry. He got away, but I'm pretty sure I *can* destroy him. Or, I mean *we* can. He didn't seem truly alive, no emotions at all… until I got a piece of him with the sword. That seemed to scare him."

"That thing killed the Devil. It damn sure better kill a piece-of… inquisitor who overstepped his station." Kingsley scowled.

"You can say *shit* in front of us. We're not *little* anymore," muttered Anthony. "I say shit all the time."

"You'd better not in front of me," I said.

"Sheesh, Mom. Like I would really do that."

"You just said it twice, idiot." Tammy tossed an empty plastic bottle at him, bouncing it off his head.

"It's okay when you're making a point."

"What point?"

"That it's okay to say shit around us—oh, shit! Oops!"

I nearly laughed but the mom in me was strong. I told Anthony to settle down and Tammy to never call her brother an idiot again. That done, I caught Allison's eye and we both snickered.

Kingsley twisted around to smile at the back seat. "I was censoring myself for innocent ears." He indicated Allison with a nod.

She picked her eye with a middle finger, making him laugh.

"So… the Red Rider is still out there?" Kingsley asked.

I nodded glumly. "Yeah."

He reached over and took my hand. "You okay?"

"Frustrated, but otherwise, yeah. More pissed than anything. I really, *really* want to kill that son of a bitch."

"Is 'son of a bitch' an insult if someone's mom is a werewolf?" asked Anthony.

Kingsley cackled. "No, it's a statement of fact."

Tammy and Allison sighed. Kingsley chuckled.

"Allie," I asked. "Did that girl actually do anything with that light show?"

"I think so, yes. She strengthened the link you have to the Red Rider. At least, making it a much more effective tracking tool. I think you've got a couple days, a week at most, before it wears off. But, in that time, you should be able to feel a stronger pull toward him."

"I got nothing. Not even a twitch."

Allison rubbed her temples in thought.

I started the engine, backed out of the driveway, and proceeded to head home. Kingsley preferred to drive, and usually did so. He never outright told me that it was a 'man's job' to drive, but that's the impression I got from him. Kingsley had, after all, grown up in a far different time with far different social mores. Still, I liked driving, even if Kingsley did make liberal use of the 'oh, shit' handle. Hey, my driving wasn't *that* bad.

Hmmph, came Tammy's voice in my head.

"He's gotta be on a different plane," said Allison about ten minutes later.

"Quite possible. That's why he's been such a bitch to find. He keeps going up the dimensional ladder... past where even angels can get to."

Tammy scrunched her eyebrows. "If angels work for God, how can that monster go higher than them? Shouldn't they be able to get closer?"

I shrugged. "I have no idea how any of that works, just that I somehow have to find a way to chase him across multiple dimensions... oh, and if I stay too long out of the one I belong in, I start to disintegrate."

"Eww," said Tammy. "Disintegration sucks."

"Mom…" Anthony squeezed my shoulder from behind. "Don't do anything crazy, okay?"

I can't tell if he's kidding or serious.

"Have you been paying attention to like *anything* lately?" asked Tammy. "Everything Mom does is crazy."

"Okay. Crazier than normal," he said, sounding far too much like an adult for my liking.

"If crazy has become normal, how do we define crazier than crazy?" asked Allison.

"That's a lot of crazy," said Kingsley from the front seat.

Tammy sighed hard while Anthony laughed.

Minutes later, the word 'crazy,' which had become lodged in my subconscious, made me think of some of the weirdos I'd run into during my career. This one guy… A HUD property I used to be responsible for got burned down by a guy who thought his girl cheated with some other man who lived in that house. Dudes do weird things when they're in love. I randomly think of Van Gogh cutting off his ear.

… and the fairy cloud taking on his image…

Wait… What? Why? Yeah, that should've meant something, but I'd been kinda fixated on a missing and soon-to-be-gruesomely-murdered child. At least I stopped that from happening. Having been denied Annie, the Red Rider would likely grab another kid soon though, of that I was certain. Considering Annie's strength, he may go after her again. Hopefully, however long it takes him to lick that wound I gave him is enough for me to catch up to him. Damn good thing Annie's got a strong spirit. I can't even imagine what must've been going through her mind while lying there alone in the cave, unable to move, starving, no water, knowing she would be killed.

And the bastard got away.

Into that box.

... which looked like an *impressionist* painting inside.

Van Gogh did impressionist work.

A sudden thought leapt into my mind... the demon-possessed artist gave me a painting that looked an awful damn lot like a Van Gogh, but none that had acquired any fame. A lost Van Gogh? Shit! I started to accelerate but remembered my kids were in the car, so I forced myself to—mostly—follow the speed limit.

14.

I ran through the house to the painting in question as soon as we got home.

Talos seemed to think that Van Gogh might be a creator who potentially achieved immortality by painting himself over and over again. But, as far as I knew, he died in his thirties after an unsuccessful suicide attempt. Shot himself in the chest or something, didn't die right away... succumbing a day or so later to an infection. Hmm. I wonder if that was every bit as much of a cover story as the FBI believing some crazy woodland hermit kidnapped Annie. If Van Gogh had given up on the third dimension and wanted to go higher, he'd have to come up with a cover story. Or maybe his relatives filled that stuff in after he disappeared. The dude supposedly suffered from serious depression, so it's likely he didn't really care what he left behind.

The more I stared at that painting, the more I began to see the man as Jeffcock. Argh. I can't think that name with a straight face. J.C. Right. My in-another-life dad, and vampire sire to boot. Yeah, guys do strange things for love all right, and not just romantic love. Seeking out a vampire, asking to be made immortal, and spending five centuries hunting down the guy who killed your daughter. Yeah. Neither my dad in this lifetime nor Danny would've done anything of the sort for me, or even our kids. Well... maybe at one time. My ex-husband did, after all, begin dabbling in dark mysticism in search of a way to get his wife back. Because, you know, Samantha Moon died that night in Hillcrest Park and I'm really just some monster who looked, talked, sounded, and thought like her. He *did* love me deeply, but couldn't handle losing me. Even though he hadn't actually lost me.

Maybe I should've kept the vampire thing secret from him after all. He clearly did not handle it well.

Anyway...

The girl in the painting has to be Daisy. J.C.'s letter mentioned they'd lived together for 'many years' after the wife died. I'd been seeing her in my mind's eye as around eighteen to twenty based on that, but the girl in this painting looked about Tammy's age. Clearly a teen on the older end of teen. Definitely not a ten-year-old. Either Annie is unusually powerful, or the Red Rider is desperate and willing to pluck an unripe witchy fruit rather than waiting for it to be ready.

Here's hoping it's option two and he's weak.

"What?" asked Kingsley, sidling up alongside me. "You think there's something to this painting?"

"There has to be. I'm sure it's a Van Gogh. He must've painted it years ago."

"I think you're being too hopeful. It looks fresh." He tapped at it. "I'm no art expert, but I've heard somewhere that it takes oils years to fully set and this doesn't seem like it's reached that point. I can still smell the paint."

"I'm sure he did."

"But Van Gogh is dead, Sam."

I glanced at Kingsley. "Is he? He kept painting self-portraits. If he's a creator, it's possible he achieved some measure of immortality, or at least a far longer than normal lifespan by constantly inserting himself into his creations. Perhaps he lives on? Or maybe he *did* die here on Earth, and one of the many various iterations of himself that he made in the other dimensions are still there."

"I didn't think LSD worked on vampires." Kingsley grinned.

"You know I'm serious."

"Yes, and you know everything you said right now just went straight over my furry canine head. I like to keep things simple and grounded."

"Oh, practicing law is simple?"

"Compared to dimension hopping and alternate

planes, it is."

"Okay. That's a fair point." I reached toward the painting. "I keep running into references to Van Gogh. I don't know if he has anything specifically to do with what's going on here, but it feels like the Universe is nudging me in this direction."

I expected to feel the texture of layered oil paint under my fingertips.

I did not expect to have an invisible force grab me and hurl me forward.

Screaming in surprise, I flew headfirst into a blinding haze of greenery. The next thing I knew, I found myself in a fairy tale forest, only everything looked way bizarre. Ever see those performance artists who literally paint people so they look like they're in oil paintings? Yeah. That world was around me now. The trees, rocks, grass, everything I could see looked like I'd physically entered an oil painting with strong impressionist leanings. Including my body. I lost a moment gawking at my hands.

Great. I'd wound up in a painter's version of the music video for *Take On Me*. If guys start chasing me with pipe wrenches, I'm going to have an issue.

"Tis a lovely day, is't not?" asked a young female voice up ahead. "My animals shall beest hither lief. I behold fia to their company."

"It doest me valorous to see thee in such high spirits, daughter," replied a man.

Oh, what the hell is going on? With no better

ideas, I advanced at a light jog toward the voices.

"Father, I doth thee heareth yond rustle in the woods. Seemeth mine furry cater-cousins has't cometh early?"

I soon reached the end of the trees where the woods met a smallish clearing with rolling meadow, a placid stream, flowers… and two painting-people. The man appeared to be in his later thirties, the young woman maybe sixteen or seventeen. Again, I looked around at the surreal scenery. Everything still appeared to be a painting.

"Excuse me. I think I'm a bit lost." I smiled.

"Oh, ill fortune, traveler. Worry not as thou art safe hither. T'is most wondrous to maketh thy acquaintance. I am Jeffcock and this is mine daughter, Daisy."

"Valorous day, Miss." The girl nodded in greeting.

"Oh… shit. I just went straight off the deep end, didn't I?"

The two exchanged glances.

"Father, wherefore doest this mistress speaketh in such a strange manner?"

Yeah.

Crap.

I've wound up staring at myself from 500 years ago.

I pointed two fingers at J.C. "You're *not* gonna believe this."

15.

It took me a few minutes to wrap my brain around what my senses tried to tell it.

Fact one: I'd somehow gone *into* a painting.

Fact two: Standing in front of me were my once-father and once-self, Daisy.

Fact three: I had a strong sense that I no longer existed within the third dimension.

Fact four: I never could read Shakespeare without getting a headache, much less listen to it.

Of course, fact three gave me a time limit. Though, I couldn't quite tell if I'd ended up in the fourth or merely a pocket nestled in the third, like the world of Dur. I'd try to figure out where Dur existed on the 'ladder' so to speak, but one, I didn't have that kind of time and two, I didn't want to go insane. Talos had a really good point as to why humans were stuck on the third dimension. We like it there. Thinking too much about beyond that is painful. I mean for heck's sake, I can sum up the reason we aren't ready for the *fourth* dimension yet (much less higher) in two words: *Duck Dynasty*.

When a bunch of backwoods dudes blasting birds out of the air was more popular than science and art? Yeah… my dragon companion's notion of it being roughly a hundred thousand years before humans were ready for more than three dimensions sounds about right, if not a bit generous.

But, back to that time-wasting thing. I'm either going to disintegrate if I stay in here too long, or the Red Rider is going to hurt someone else… most likely before I can find them. My becoming involved in the Annie situation was a stroke of pure luck. I can't roll those dice again.

Before I could think of anything to ask these people, my brain got stuck trying to figure out if they *were* people. Clearly, Daisy, my former pre-reincarnation by several lifetimes self, had been murdered. From the look of her, probably not long from now. Crap. That pissed me off even more to find out I'd been so young. Sixteen is still a child to me. That's a year younger than Tammy, and the thought that someone murdered a kid that age made my blood boil.

Oh, I *totally* understood why J.C. did what he did.

He seemed to pick up on the meaning in the

look I gave him.

"Prithee, allow me a moment to confer with the mistress in confidence, sweet Daisy. Matters not suit'd to a babe of thy tender age."

"Father, thee coddle me too much, but on this I relent as thee so wish. I will beest close, ov'r thither." Daisy gestured at the stream and wandered off. No sooner did she percheth—I mean perch—beside the water than an army of small woodland creatures came out to her.

Cripes. The girl was a veritable Disney movie. *I* was a veritable Disney movie.

"Samantha," said J.C. "It's so good to see you."

I blinked at his sudden shift in language. "Yeah. Why did you stop talking like a Shakespearean play?"

"I am who you think I am and I have lived through many years. As one who spends a long time in a new place often does, I have picked up the dialect."

"Wait. Are you…"

"Neither alive, dead, undead, nor your sire." He flashed a confusing smile. "I am a simulacrum of all of those things, but truly none. In this world, I am real. In your world, I am fiction. But what is reality but the experiences fed to one's mind? I am no less genuine than anyone you are accustomed to in the third dimension."

"You know about the whole dimension thing, too? Why am I the last one to find everything out?"

He laughed. "I know what you know because I am still a vampire, your sire, and know your mind."

"You're my sire, but not my sire?"

"Exactly."

"My brain's on fire."

J.C. 2.0 chuckled. "To put it in a way you might better understand, it is quite possible for two nearby parallel dimensions to contain near exact copies of various people, concepts, even objects. A Jeffcock existed in the third dimension five centuries prior to your time there. I existed here in parallel to him. We are the same, yet not."

"So, like twins?"

"That fails to adequately encompass it, but perhaps it will need to suffice, lest we waste precious time with a belabored explanation that will ultimately prove to be pointless."

"Is Daisy going to…?"

"No. Not this version of her. You would do well to think of her as a fictional recreation. The way a character in a book is always there, unchanging, each time you read it. I believe we have existed here for many years, yet she is still a girl of sixteen. I would not have been a vampire at this point in my life in your world, yet here I am. Perhaps the Red Rider avoids Daisy here for he fears me in this form. When he took her third-dimensional self, I would have been helpless to stop him."

I sighed. "Well, that makes me feel somewhat better, that she won't die. So, she's stuck here forever?"

We both looked over at her at the same time.

Daisy, or whatever this girl happened to be, sat in the grass by the water, surrounded by rabbits, baby deer, mice, birds, chipmunks... the whole nine. They all climbed over her, perched in her hair, and even appeared to be talking to her. Watching this triggered an upwelling of envy and anger. As with Annie, I didn't have any ill feelings toward this girl, merely a sense of longing at what had been taken away from me in my lifetime. And anger at the Red Rider.

I already had plenty of that, but hey, there's always room for Jell-O... or in this case jealousy.

To break my spiral of negative emotions, I pictured Judge Judy reaming out the Red Rider in her courtroom for preying on young girls. Ooh. Compared to that, maybe ramming the Devil Killer into his heart would be letting him off easy.

Still, I couldn't help but feel a bit like a part of me had been taken away, and I mourned it, wanted it. Maybe I *had* really seen a fairy when I'd been a little girl. And I allowed my sadness at being poor, worry about being teased at school for being from 'the poor hippie family' and all that associated bullshit to drag my thoughts away from the fanciful.

I also expected Elizabeth to make a snide comment at catching me feeling maudlin, missing the magic that had been taken from me, but she surprisingly didn't open her non-mouth. I would've said something about her being smart to keep quiet, but no sense poking a sleeping bear with a stick when I can ignore her.

"Stuck isn't exactly the best term. Neither she nor I have any sense of being trapped or wanting to be elsewhere. This is our world, perhaps at the happiest it had been for her after my wife died."

"Wait, if you're a vampire, how are you out in the sun?"

He smiled. "How are you?"

I held up the ring.

"I am simultaneously a vampire and not. Perhaps that is why. Or I simply choose not to care about the sun."

"Oh, wouldn't that be nice." I sighed wistfully. Watching Daisy interact with the animals warmed my heart despite making me feel even more like the kid no one picked in gym class. An outsider. "How did you come to be here like this? Doesn't reliving the same day over and over again drive you mad?"

"It isn't the same day, it's the same moment, the same period in our lives. Think of it like days passing but neither of us grow older. A creator captured this point in time, preserving it for eternity."

"Van Gogh."

J.C. bowed his head and nodded.

"How did he even know to paint you like this?" I wracked my brain trying to understand. Alternate worlds, multiple stacked dimensions, all of it overwhelmed me to think about. Yet, the Red Rider had escaped via that strange box. The world inside it looked much like my present surroundings, painted.

"That, I'm afraid is beyond my knowledge." J.C. sighed.

"Are you and Daisy the only people here? How far does this forest go?"

"As far as it ought to. The town is still there where I left it. My daughter much prefers the quiet solitude out here. I imagine the whole world—or perhaps a version thereof—exists here."

Hmm. They say artists create whole worlds, but I didn't think *they* meant to be quite so literal about it. "If the Red Rider found Van Gogh somehow and exploited… wait!" My eyes widened in realization. "He's like a hub or something. All those paintings could act like the spokes of a wheel, pathways to different dimensions."

J.C. furrowed his brow. "I'm afraid I do not know much of this rider, only what I am able to see in your mind through our link. Yet, I feel as though I should."

"The reason you hunted him hasn't happened yet in this timeline. Perhaps it won't because this isn't really a timeline as much as an alternate world with alternate versions of you and Daisy in it."

"I'd say that wouldn't explain how I am presently a vampire and know I sired you, but I am sure you have more pressing things to attend to than unwinding a Mobius strip of intra-dimensional logic."

"I've more pressing things to do than unwinding whatever you just said."

He laughed.

"If I'm right, and Van Gogh is the nexus… there must be something here. I need to go."

"Of course." J.C. bowed. "May you find what you seek."

I thanked him and ran off into the woods. My theory didn't make much sense, but then again, I'd gone inside a painting. That didn't make much sense either, at least in terms of what most normal people would consider 'making sense.' I had no idea where to go or what exactly to look for. Perhaps following my gut would pan out...

16.

An hour—as best I could estimate—later, the distant *thump, thump, thump* of a heartbeat emerged from the placid sounds of the wild.

I couldn't quite tell if I really heard it or imagined it, but I decided to go toward it. The pulsing never became as loud as it had been in the cave where I'd found Annie, but I continued walking toward the source of the sound until I reached a pastoral clearing. Pale green meadow grass lined a swath of open terrain speckled with flowers of yellow and red. White butterflies darted around, dancing to the trill of unseen birds.

A man in oldish clothing sat on a sizable boulder beside an easel. The canvas waited for his brush, blank and filled with limitless possibility. He stood out from the environment as he constantly shifted back and forth from appearing painted to photographic. Or, I should say, normal, like any other person from my three-dimensional world. His body shifted in an ever-changing swarm of colored lines that faded to standard humanity and returned, like the Eighties music video I'd wandered into had decided to go trippy.

At my approach, the man turned to look at me, revealing a bandage over his right ear.

Holy shit. Van Gogh!

"Hello, Samantha," said the artist.

"You know me?"

"Of course. You are in my world. You could not exist here if I didn't know you."

I walked up to stand beside him. Admittedly, looking at the bright paint lines squiggling in and vanishing so rapidly hurt my eyes, but I didn't want to flinch away for fear of offending him. "Can you help me find the… creature known as the Red Rider?"

"Perhaps. The entity of which you speak has been trespassing in my realms for a long time. Though, he does no real harm here, merely tramples through crushing flowers."

"He's been murdering innocent girls for centuries."

Van Gogh grimaced. "So sad. There is so much sadness in the world. Tis why I left."

"Do you know where he is? Not sure why I'm asking you… the angels can't even locate him."

"He goes to what you would refer to as the fifth dimension."

"How does he survive there?"

"I know not. I create worlds; I do not take them apart to see the gears."

"What's with the box, the heartbeat?"

"Box?" His eyebrows crept up. "Oh. That. The entity you seek constructed it. He destroyed one of my paintings and used the canvas to line the monstrosity. It is something of an anchor for him."

"Grr. So I should've jumped into the box after him. Dammit."

"That may have placed you right… what is the phrase, 'on his tail?' but you would not have been prepared for the transition in frequency, which could have left you vulnerable."

"I need to find him. Can you help?"

Van Gogh turned back to his empty canvas. "I'm afraid I'm waiting for the muse to speak to me."

I furrowed my brows. Okay, time to play the muse.

"Mr. Van Gogh?"

He looked up at me.

With a smile, I gave his brain a subtle poke. He found me entrancing and wanted to paint a scene of me. The sparkle in his eyes told me my suggestion caught on. He sprang to his feet and walked about ten paces away where he arranged me to stand under a tree, reaching up toward a flower on a branch. I put up with his posing requirements, seeing as how he appeared to be the key to my pursuit of the Red Rider. The last time he made eye contact before returning to the canvas, I further prodded him with a desire to paint me into the fifth dimension.

Van Gogh hurried back to his canvas and got to work.

Being undead did wonders for my ability to hold still. Soon after he started, I remembered Kingsley's admonition not to run off alone... so I filled Van Gogh's head with images of him, Allison... and my kids. Part of me hesitated at including Tammy and Anthony, but I could no longer deny that both of them had come into power in their own right. Neither remained helpless children in need of protection. The Fire Warrior was a serious badass, and if any being in the universe could get into the Rider's head, Tammy could. Then again, maybe she *shouldn't* look in there. My daughter could barely handle what I imagined he did to those girls. Seeing the truth would break her. Still, she could help in other ways, like sharing ideas among us that he couldn't hear or react to. Or maybe even forcing ideas into his head instead of reading, perhaps even confusing and disorienting him.

That, and I didn't want to leave her alone.

Van Gogh flew into a frenzy of waving arms. I hoped time passed differently in this world than mine, as it felt like many hours passed before he finally sagged back to sit on the boulder, out of breath with a look of... Well, let's just say the last time I saw that expression on a man's face, Kingsley wore it and we lay in bed together, both quite exhausted.

I resisted the urge to make a 'was it good for you, too' joke, and walked over to check out the painting. It caught me off guard mostly because it looked nothing at all like the scene I'd posed for. He hadn't even included the tree. Rather than stand there like some young French girl with nothing better to do than wander the countryside in summer, he'd painted me standing in the pose of a warrior maiden, my wings out, the Devil Killer held at the ready. A cluster of small animals gathered around my feet, staring up at me with adoration in their eyes. Also, the tiny figure of a faerie stood on my shoulder, in much the same pose as an admiral on the bridge of a battleship heading into war.

Kingsley, Allison, Tammy, and Anthony stood around me, all striking dramatic poses like the cover of an epic fantasy novel. Only our modern clothing broke the vibe. The background exploded in vibrant colors, fuchsia-leafed trees, a green sky with indigo clouds, plants of no kind I'd ever seen before, all covered in fuzzy puffs of pastel blue or yellow. In the distance to the rear left, the silvery gleam of a futuristic metropolis radiated light. Opposite it, the sky darkened, suggesting that way led to a bog or mire.

Great. He painted the cover for *National Lampoons goes to Krull* or something. Left turn, utopia city. Right turn, the swamp of evil. Something tells me I know where I'll be headed. Ugh. I also got the sense that touching the painting would have the same effect that touching the one back home did... pull me in.

"Do you know how long I have before I start to disintegrate?"

"Not terribly long, I'm afraid." Van Gogh offered a sad smile. "However, I will do what I can to protect you."

"How?"

"Repairing the painting as it fades. But that will only give you *more* time, as I cannot continue to paint forever. You will need to return home as fast as you are able."

"Thank you. I understand."

One of the rabbits he'd added near my foot appeared to be staring at me out from the painting as if alive. In fact, the whole canvas felt more like an opening into elsewhere than a flat image.

Here goes nothing.

I reached out and gently touched the painting...

17.

With a brilliant flash, the impressionist forest around me changed into the vibrant otherworld in the painting. The scattering of animals gathered around me took only seconds to 'drink me in' before they decided to run like hell. Can't say I blamed them, I am, after all, undead. It still kinda hurt though.

Oh well.

Kingsley, Allison, Tammy, and Anthony all stared at me. For an instant, I felt incredibly glad that the creator in question was Van Gogh and not, say, Raphael or Boris Vallejo—or we'd all be mostly naked... and probably rippling with ridiculous muscles.

"Oh, wow, that worked," I said on a whispery breath.

"What worked?" asked Tammy.

"Are you guys really here or are you like J.C. and Daisy from the other painting... some kind of copies?"

"Mom." Anthony put a hand on my arm. "There's this guy at school who does a presentation about drugs. I think you should listen to him."

Tammy scoffed. "She's not on drugs, butthead. She's just not making any sense."

"She's making sense." Allison looked around. "It's just a topic that melts down most normal brains... like that movie *Inception*."

"Ugh." Tammy shivered. "That one gave me a headache."

"I liked it." Anthony shrugged.

"That's because you didn't get it enough to understand that you didn't understand it."

"Dork alert," said Anthony.

I blinked. Okay, maybe Van Gogh didn't make copies and somehow brought them here for real. Or they're really damn good copies. Either way, I kept my promise to Kingsley. I wasn't going to charge in alone.

"Pink leaves are a nice touch." Allison whistled in awe. "This place is wild."

"Actually, I think that's fuchsia." Kingsley scratched behind his ear.

"What's fuchsia?" asked Anthony.

"Pink for hipsters." Tammy folded her arms.

Kingsley feigned offense.

As I turned in place looking around, a bizarre feeling scraped over my awareness. The direction remained constant regardless of how I faced, like I stood at the corner of a building and rubbed against it while spinning.

"Guys." I pointed in the direction that matched—sure enough at the dark place in the distance. "I'm getting a weird feeling from that way."

"Yeah. It's called 'don't go to the Forest of Total Creepiness.'" Tammy shook her head. "You know every character in every horror movie sees something scary and messed up and yet they still go there."

"We're not in a horror movie," I said. "And you saw Annie. I have to stop that bastard."

Tammy, uncharacteristically meek, leaned against me with a 'not too overt for public' hug. "Yeah. We gotta."

"I should have my head examined bringing you two with me to a place like that." I sighed. "I fail at momming."

"Nah." Anthony patted me on the back. "Child services won't take us away from you." He waited a moment. "You'd just mind control them."

"Heh. Funny." I glanced at him. "*True*. But funny."

"Okay." Allison waved her hand around, summoning a few scraps of dancing light, which orbited my head. "Yeah. Annie's magic is working.

I'm sure you're feeling the Red Rider's trail. What she did made the link you have with him much stronger. Enough that it's probably a physical sensation."

"Yeah. And it's pulling me *that* way."

"Of course it is," muttered Tammy. "Into the deep dark woods."

"What?" Anthony shrugged. "You expected a monster who tortures and kills young witches to live in a little pink house full of kitten pictures or something?"

She gave him the side eye. "No. The Red Rider isn't *that* evil."

"Come on," I said. "We don't have all the time in the world."

I hurried along a quaint dirt footpath toward the Forest of Woe… or whatever the place was called. Surely it had a name somewhere in the depths of Van Gogh's mind.

We walked past fields of grass, both green as well as teal with azure patches. Flowers with bizarre repeating geometric shapes like something out of an MC Escher painting leaned closer to us as we passed, as if alive and curious.

"The tulips are looking at me," said Anthony.

I glanced back a moment later to find Allison fifty or so feet behind us, staring into one of those flowers, mesmerized.

"Don't look into the flowers!" I half yelled, then ran back to grab Allison's arm.

She snapped out of it, blinking. "Whoa. That was trippy. Felt like I was staring into a Mandelbrot zoom. Just endless repeating fractals."

The trail continued into woods composed of black-trunked trees with pale blue needles.

"Heh. Emo pines," said Tammy.

"If they had fur, would they be Lou Pines?" asked Anthony.

Kingsley groaned.

"You're adopted," said Tammy. "Please tell me he's adopted."

I hugged them both. "Nope."

We passed a small pond of glowing water. 'Fish' that resembled partially inflated balloons with eyes and tiny little flapper fins that blurred like hummingbird wings zoomed around like overcaffeinated Pomeranians. They looked part goofy and part cute, but when I started toward them, my alarm sense blared strong... as though they could legit kill me.

"Stay back!" I grabbed my kids. "Those fish are bad news."

Everyone looked at me like I'd gone nuts, except Kingsley. He, too, had an inner alarm, although I always suspected mine was a little more far reaching. Still, if his triggered... then, yeah, this was bad news.

"Listen to your mother," he said in a low voice. "Not everything that looks cute is harmless." He smiled. "Take your mom for example."

"Eww," deadpanned Tammy.

Allison giggled. "Aww, you guys."

I gave his hand a squeeze, but also walked faster. I loved spending time with everyone here, but alas, time was one thing we presently didn't have much of. Both because the Rider would recover his power eventually and prey on another innocent, and because we would all disintegrate. Already, I noticed parts of my body—as well as everyone else's—fading semitransparent for seconds at a time before solidity smeared back over the opening as if by brush stroke.

Van Gogh, a dimension or two… up or down? Ugh. I have no idea. Anyway, he obviously still sat by that painting and kept fixing the damage. Seeing everyone else disintegrate as well got me worrying that they had really come through into this world with me, not simulacrums like J.C. and Daisy.

"How'd you guys get here?" I asked out of the blue, while gazing around at the massive black trees, as tall as high-rises.

"When you slurped into the painting, Anthony tried to grab you," said Tammy. "He got pulled in after you. Kingsley told me not to, but I went after him."

He sighed. "And then I followed."

"Party of one is boring," chirped Allison. "So here I am, too."

"We all ended up in a forest that looked like a Van Gogh painting, said Kingsley. "No sign of you, but we found each other reasonably soon. Wandered for a bit, then this doorway opened and we saw you on the other side, so we stepped through." Kingsley sniffed the air. "This place is playing hell with my nose."

"What's it smell like?" asked Allison.

"Yes."

"It smells like 'yes'?" Anthony blinked. "What does that even mean?"

Kingsley chuckled. "It's too intense to describe. Like everything at once but nothing."

"You *are* a hipster." Tammy rolled her eyes. "That was so esoteric it hurts."

"Esoteric! Like *that's* really a word," snorted Anthony.

His sister was about to reply—no doubt derisively—when a bluish-white glow from ahead caught my attention.

"Shh," I said, raising a hand. "I see something."

Everyone quieted and followed me as I crept forward. Past a grove of massive trees, these coated in a glowing orange lichen, stood an energy bubble the size of a compact car. Well, I assumed it to be an energy bubble. It might've been a crystal ball, though I'd never seen one six feet around before. Inside, the distorted image of a city appeared, but shifted back and forth, trading places with a barren field where something dark lurked in the distance. I couldn't place the city, but it appeared modern and third-dimensional. My link to the Red Rider pulsed stronger the closer I moved to it.

"Whoa," whispered Allison.

"You could say that again," I said. "But don't."

"Whoa," she said.

"Bitch."

Tammy reached out to touch the ball, but I caught her hand.

"Wait a sec, hon."

She shot me a look like the sarcasm cannon was primed, but must've picked up the worry in my heart for her safety, so she didn't fire it.

"This is definitely connected to him somehow." I walked around the giant ball. "I think it might be that dimensional anchor I was thinking of. This could be the other end of the box, or maybe it's some manner of bridge between frequencies."

Kingsley shot me a strained expression. Right. I shouldn't burden werewolf brains with arcane metaphysics.

Tammy giggled.

I thought about touching it and no warning sense went off in my head, so I gingerly reached out and rested my hand on a perfectly smooth ice cold surface. At that, Tammy did the same. Nothing happened other than a potent tingle of energy sweeping over the back of my hand, and I imagined, hers, too.

"Yeah. It tingles," said Tammy.

"That's what she said," muttered Anthony.

Tammy gasped and blushed.

"Anthony!" I stared at him. "That's your sister."

Kingsley snickered.

"I didn't mean *her*." My son rolled his eyes. "Jeez, Mom, it's just a joke to say that."

I spent a few minutes mentally feeling out the giant crystal ball. The sense that Annie empowered me with, rather the sense I had that the kid made stronger, pulled me upward. Somehow, I doubted it meant flying literally straight up from here. One of the two images in the ball looked like normal Earth, so I assumed the other one to be a higher dimension. Maybe sixth since it didn't appear *too* different from my present surroundings. Though, it lacked the color, being rather gloomy and drab.

"There's a way to activate this thing." Allison rested both her hands on it, gazing far into its depths. "I think the easiest way to describe it is an elevator. Only, instead of traversing floors, it's hopping realities."

"We're gonna be late getting home for dinner, aren't we?" asked Anthony, scratching his stomach. "Can we get pizza?"

The only hunger in this world greater than the Red Rider's thirst for power is a teenage boy's hunger for… pizza, chicken nuggets, fries, or whatever else comes within arm's reach that isn't considered 'healthy.'

"Any idea how to make this ball work?" asked Kingsley. "Maybe if we rub it something will happen."

Tammy glared at Anthony, commanding him

not to make another 'that's what she said' joke.

My son *does* know when to keep his mouth shut... sometimes.

"Working on it." Allison muttered about prodding and pulling at magical energy threads. That I didn't understand her annoyed me, even though it shouldn't have. I'm not a witch.

Not anymore, whispered Elisabeth. *We're not so different, Sssamantha. You know what it is like to be deprived of something that belongs to you by right.*

Oh? And what exactly belongs to you by right that was taken away?

The world.

I rolled my eyes. Not even the same thing. You want to dominate people, control everything. No one gave you the world. Magic belonged to me by bloodline, for generations. It should've been mine. I should have...

I glanced over at Allison, struck by a sudden pang of sadness that I couldn't fulfill the role fate had set me on a path toward. I stood on the outside while some other woman stole my rightful place in the trifecta. Hell, my best friend had to block me out of her mind.

Elizabeth receded again, and I felt her smiling to herself. Ooh. Bitch. I never should've thought about feeling cheated. Now she's going to be holding that over me for the rest of time.

An inkling of thought formed in my head for no particular reason, growing into an understanding of how to focus on the orb to activate it. I've never studied magic in any form, but somehow—maybe via the link I shared with the Red Rider, I received some kind of psychic hit that read his thoughts at the moment he used it. Kind of like the way some psychics can pick up a murder weapon and see the crime. Or maybe it came from Elizabeth. The understanding grew and took shape in my mind...

"No way that makes any sense," said Tammy, cringing, and shooting a look from me to Allison.

Except my friend blinked... and smiled. "Oh but I do. It's so complicated yet so simple. I should've thought of that."

"Wait. You understood that?" asked Tammy, gobsmacked.

"Yeah. It's like rather basic in fundamental theory, even though it appears hella complicated." Allison looked over at me. "Ready?"

"Yeah." I placed both hands against the orb. "Everyone get close to us."

As they did so, Kingsley said, "Wait! Maybe we shouldn't trust sudden flashes of inspiration like that. Something wanted you to know that. And nothing is ever free."

"Or what if I read the Red Rider's mind by his link to this object?"

Kingsley narrowed his eyes at me.

"Is your danger sense going off?" I asked.

"Not really." He grumbled.

"Mine isn't either." I nodded at Allison. "You

ready?"

"Yeppers."

"Please don't say yeppers again."

"I second that," said Tammy.

And before Allison could say it again, I pushed my right hand up, left hand down, twisting. Despite lacking any magical ability, I flexed my brain in a manner that I imagined a witch or warlock might when invoking spells or manipulating magical energy.

The crystal orb swelled up to many times its size, engulfing us. Two seconds later, it collapsed, pulling us inward with shoving force. A brief flash occurred, and we appeared in midair, a frightening distance above a barren, tundra field. On the left, a long strip of grey mountains lined the horizon. To the right, ahead, and rear, the empty land stretched as far as I could see. It took me a second to realize we were fairly high up—and falling...

18.

Reflexively, I sprouted my angel wings and reached for my kids. Anthony burst into the Fire Warrior, growing too large—and hot—for me to carry. I grabbed Tammy, who clamped onto me like a koala bear. I hurled myself into a power dive and caught Allison.

Kingsley shifted into his werewolf form seconds before hitting the ground. The fall probably wouldn't have been fatal to a normal human, but it would've meant broken bones. He landed with relative grace, the greatly increased strength of his shifted form allowing his muscles to absorb the impact with minimal effort.

From the air, I spotted a dark-walled castle built against the mountains a fair distance away. At my thought of 'hmm. Probably should just fly there,'

Tammy clung tighter and shivered. I glided lower to the ground to calm her fear of heights, and skimmed along maybe ten feet above sparse grass and dirt. Allison's hair whipped me in the face as she looked around awestruck.

Anthony followed us, running over the land in great strides, hurtling smaller trees and chasms, up and over hillsides with mind boggling speed. Meanwhile, Allison didn't seem to mind either the height or being carried. If anything, she seemed focused on my son, who was a sight to behold, to be sure.

Mom?

Yes?

Allison is having creepy thoughts about Anthony. She thinks he's like hunky or something. Eww.

I smirked. Allison is having 'thoughts' about the Fire Warrior. The body she's fantasizing about is not technically Anthony.

Much like Talos, I suspected my son was only borrowing that body. Who or whatever the actual being is, I'm still not entirely sure.

Okay. That's a lot less gross to think about—and don't you dare!

Damn. She heard me wondering if I flew a little higher if I could get her to spill the beans about her possible new boyfriend. Of course I wouldn't really terrify my little girl by flying higher and higher to extort information from her. Nah. That would be mean.

"Not funny," whimpered Tammy.

Kingsley sprinted on all fours, a black streak of fur zooming over the dying grass, keeping pace with my son the fire warrior.

With the fear of imminent splat gone, I finally took in my surroundings. No longer did the world have a strange painterly quality. Everything looked beyond perfect. Seeing this reality around me felt like the first time looking at high definition television—only this went beyond the sharpness of mere high-def. Every ridge or crinkle in the distant mountains appeared crisp enough to slice paper. Every cloud above so fluffy they resembled levitating cotton puffs. Individual blades of grass fluttered in such extreme detail I couldn't help but picture Anthony raving about the awesome graphics processing power of his new game system.

Kingsley slowed, gazing at me for direction, and continued following along behind me, close enough that he could've leapt up and grabbed me out of the air. Anthony, in turn, followed him. Upon reaching a thin dirt road flecked with white stones, I swung my body upright and landed, setting Allison down first. Tammy hugged me in thanks for being back on the ground, and let go.

Anthony landed beside me and surveyed the area with his fists on his hips. Despite the horror of what the Red Rider did, and the urgency I felt to eliminate him, my son seemed to be adoring this. Like he was a character in one of his video games.

He's scared too, said Tammy in my head. *But,*

yeah, he thinks he's Conan or something.

I smirked. Well, he basically is at the moment. Or at least has Conan's body on layaway.

If Conan was fifteen-feet tall and on fire.

"Wow, everything looks so... so... vibrant here." Allison whistled. "It's almost painful to look at anything."

"I can count individual grains of dirt," said Kingsley, after shifting back to his human form. He dropped to a knee and lowered his face to the ground, sniffing, then looked toward the distant castle. "I believe the entity we're chasing passed by here recently. Leather, blood, and... a sulfurous foulness."

"Demon? He's part demon?" I asked.

"Not entirely. But he has touched the same energies they used. Perhaps he has absorbed those who trafficked with them and taken that energy?"

Anthony shifted his large head to stare at Tammy with a purposeful glint in his flaming eyes.

"He's wondering if this thing absorbed evil witches and they made him turn evil."

I shrugged. "Maybe." Although it did seem unlikely. Not too many young witches would have gone dark at such an early age, but who knew?

"Or," said Allison, "maybe creatures as evil as this bastard just stink."

"I like her theory." I marched forward.

"Explain Anthony's underwear," muttered Tammy.

"There's no explanation for that," I said.

The giant Fire Warrior shot me an 'aww Mom really?' stare.

Minutes later, we reached a footpath of white gravel that led to a huge stone wall. A massive portcullis gate blocked our passage. However, being a simple wall, I flew over it. Anthony pulled himself over it like a ranch hand jumping a fence. Kingsley, back in his wolf form, sprang to the top, then dropped down past it.

I landed in a large courtyard of dark cobblestones. Hundreds of figures in hooded white robes milled around a fountain at the center. The thin material pressed to their bodies as they moved, revealing the shapes of young girls ranging in age from maybe fifteen up to their early twenties—the majority probably sixteen or seventeen. Some stood in place, others meandered about, all with vacant far-off expressions. Like everything else in this dimension, they appeared hyper-real, every pore on their faces stood out in exquisite detail. Bare feet peeked out from under the dragging hems of their robes. Hands and arms hung limp at their sides. Not one reacted to our presence.

"Whoa," whispered Allison. "This is so damn eerie."

Narrow stone stairways connected from the ground here and there to equally narrow openings in various towers around the courtyard. The expressionless girls wandered up or down, disappearing into the castle, reappearing elsewhere—or maybe those were different girls.

One, a redhead of about seventeen passed within inches of me, not acknowledging my presence at all. She radiated a charged energy that washed over me like a rain of tiny needles scratching at my skin despite my clothes. I stood in horrified awe, staring at what had to be hundreds of girls.

"Hey," said Tammy, attempting to communicate with a dark-haired girl about her age. "What's up?"

The girl walked right on by.

Anthony waved his enormous, fiery hand at a young woman trying to get her attention. She, too, ignored him.

"Oh, my God," rasped Allison. "These must be all his victims…" She looked from girl to girl for a moment, then swooned to her knees, bawling hard. "He killed them all…"

"Worse than that," muttered Tammy.

Kingsley sniffed at one as she passed him, then sneezed from the electric tingles on his hypersensitive nose. He emitted a whine and looked up at Tammy.

"He doesn't think these are true spirits," said Tammy. "I'm not entirely sure what we're looking at."

Allison kept crying.

"We're looking at the reason I'm going to end this…"

"Go ahead, Mom. Say it. This deserves an f-bomb," rasped Tammy, a hitch of sorrow in her voice.

Ssso much needless suffering, whispered Elizabeth. *Some of those children are younger than your daughter. Think on that...*

Tammy grabbed a passing girl's hand. The white-robed entity stopped walking and stood still, continuing to stare into space. My daughter pressed a hand to the other girl's chest, listened at her mouth, then backed off. All the while, the strange phantom continued walking as though nothing had happened. "She's warm, but I didn't feel a heartbeat."

I have done things most might regard as dark, but even I am aghast at such cruelty. You are right to be livid. That one over by the fountain looked like such a sweet girl. She didn't deserve to be starved, flayed, and consumed alive.

I shuddered. The girl in question, a bright blue-eyed blonde, had a young, innocent face. The sort of girl who'd cry over mice killed in traps or refuse to smash bugs in the house. She perched on the edge of a grim, ebony-colored fountain, her pale bare feet inches off the ground. Everything about her posture said she should be smiling and enjoying the beautiful day, but her expression was as blank and lifeless as the stone courtyard tiles.

The sight of her hit me with the exact opposite emotion as befell Allison. Inside, I flew into a rage. I wanted to tear the Red Rider apart. I wanted him to suffer like he'd made these young girls suffer. I really wanted him to scream. Anger took me to a place so far away from who I was that I didn't even mind Elizabeth smiling at my rage, at my wanting to visit sheer pain upon this wretch of a being who could do such things to innocent children.

Not one looked anywhere near as young as Annie though. That truth kept me from entirely losing all rational thought to rage. Again, I wondered if the Rider had become desperate for nourishment. He'd gorged himself on magic for five centuries, and evidently, the buffet hadn't been refilled. I hoped he'd chosen to prey on such a young girl because he'd become weakened and desperate.

Use your anger, Sssamantha.

I couldn't help but smirk. Are you trying to give me encouragement or lure me to the dark side?

Tammy caught my thought. "What? Oh. Well, she might have a point, Mom. This guy is nasty. Fight fire with fire and all that. Like what you did with the Devil."

"No way this thing is more powerful than the Devil." I shook my head. "Crueler, perhaps, but not more powerful."

My daughter cringed. "Sorry again."

"What for?"

"You know… being dumb enough to fall for his crap."

I squeezed her shoulder. "You weren't dumb.

He played to your vulnerability. That's kinda who he was."

"Is," corrected Allison. "Isn't he back?"

"Sort of. At least, I'm guessing based on what I saw in that painter's house. Not so much 'back' as there's a new Devil in town."

"Better the devil you know, right?" Allison managed a sad laugh. "That's *supposed* to be a metaphor."

Kingsley emitted a wolf snort.

I crossed the courtyard of lost souls to the fountain. The eerie-ass thing, shiny and polished black, had been shaped into a twisting mass of spectral figures gathering together in a tornado of ghostly energy, their faces warped in agony.

"Cheery place," muttered Kingsley.

Allison clamp-hugged the blonde girl sitting on the fountain. The teen ignored her. After a moment, my friend finally wiped her tears and got her composure back, looking pissed all of a sudden. "Let's do this. This thing needs to die."

"Ack! Mom!" Tammy held up her hands; all her fingers had vanished. "What's happening?"

One by one, her fingers reappeared. She almost went cross-eyed staring at her hands in bewilderment.

"I am having to work faster and faster to repaint the details of your figures," said Van Gogh from the heavens. "Whatever you plan to do in there, make haste. Your time draws short."

"The only thing we can do to help these girls is to destroy the fiend that did this to them." I drew the Devil Killer from its dimensional sheath, considered my options, and did the only thing I could think of...

I charged the rest of the way across the courtyard to the castle doors.

Kingsley and Anthony bounded past me, the wolf running, Anthony's huge strides appearing slow but covering ground equally as fast. The two of them hit the door with a *boom* that shook the entire castle, or at least seemed loud enough to.

"So much for subtle," muttered Allison, coming up behind me, gasping. My daughter trailed behind her.

"We're not here to be subtle." I cautioned my daughter to stay put, then stormed inside and down a grand hallway, following a dark burgundy runner past armor statues, tapestries, and other decorations that made me think I'd walked into a Crusades-age monastery—though one low on spirituality and high on torture and murder.

The pull led me around a left turn and along another passageway to a set of ornate double doors in dark brown wood. Six stone cherubs carved upon them in bas-relief all shifted their heads to stare at me as I approached. Oh, that wasn't creepy at all. Moving wooden angel babies with creepy smiles... yeah, totally a normal thing to see.

I grabbed the handles and pulled the heavy doors apart, revealing a darkened cathedral full of crimson tapestries and paintings depicting the torture and burning of witches. A broad-shouldered figure in a hooded, crimson robe stood hunched over the altar with his back to us. The room hung in silence except for the echoing slurp of greedy feasting.

Fortunately, the Red Rider's hood didn't block my view of the altar, and it was obvious he didn't have a young girl's corpse in front of him. Still, I didn't want to know what he ate. Though, I suspected he had a stash of former victim to munch on. Tammy squeezed up next to me on the left, cringing from the gruesome décor surrounding us. This room had no pews or benches for any faithful to gather, merely a large open area filled with images of agony.

And one wretched fiend.

"You're a hard man to find." I stepped into the room.

The Red Rider whirled to stare at me, a strip of red flesh dangling from bloody teeth. Unlike our first meeting where he had all the emotional depth of an ATM kiosk, here, he appeared manic. Eyes wild with frenzy grew even wider at the sight of me. I couldn't tell if he reacted in fear, anger, or excitement, as his expression could've fit any of those.

"Now what?" whispered Allison.

"Now…" I strode toward him. "We send this piece of shit straight to hell."

19.

The Red Rider screamed out a high-pitched, keening wail.

His horse materialized beside him in a puff of dark red smoke.

"Aww. We can't hurt his poor horse," whined Tammy.

The animal raked a hoof at the floor, snarling and snorting flames from its nostrils.

"Never mind. That's not really a horse." She jumped back.

I charged the Red Rider. The horse snorted a firebolt at me, so I leapt straight up onto my wings as the glowing serpent of flame licked at the floor. Angling forward, I turned my jump into a dive, swooping down at the Rider. He raised his gladius. Our swords clashed with a *boom* that echoed over the room like thunder. My dive stalled, all my weight on the point where our weapons crossed.

The horse whirled to attack me, but vanished with a strange, strangled snarl in a blur of Fire Warrior. The Red Rider shoved me aside, but before he could swing, Kingsley, in wolf form, leapt at him. Giant werewolf teeth sank into the Rider's shoulder. Growling, he picked the inquisitor from hell up in his mouth and thrashed him side to side. The Rider stabbed Kingsley in the ribs, which only appeared to make my man angrier. It did, however, cause him to hurl the Red Rider into the air.

Allison threw magical energy at the walls, floor, and ceiling, chanting and whispering. In response to her, the doors we entered by slammed as if pulled by invisible hands. Intricate mystical patterns traced themselves into being, drawn in hairline golden threads.

After bouncing off the wall and scrambling back to his feet, the Red Rider stared at Allison... and drooled.

Oh, hell no.

"You're not devouring my friend!" I shouted, again launching myself into a wing-flapping rush, half running, half flying.

The fire-spitting horse came out of nowhere and flew over my head, upside down. I ducked the startling sight, twisting to watch it crash into the wall on the other end of the room. My son tromped after it, chasing the hellbeast he'd thrown.

Allison hurled a bolt of magical energy at the Red Rider, who'd gone running at her like a dog chasing a dropped piece of filet mignon. Her spell caught him in the chest, stalling him to an abrupt stop. I cruised in, swinging the Devil Killer. He raised his left arm, blocking my sword with the buckler shield strapped to it. My blade scorched the leather on contact, sparking and fuming.

A scream from Tammy distracted me. I got a brief glimpse of her diving to the floor to get under another fire breath from the horse before the Red Rider's gladius plunged into my gut. He yanked it out and slugged me in the jaw with his sword hand. I held my ground, barely yielding a single step.

He stared at me, aghast that a woman my size didn't go flying over backward… or seem to care much about an abdominal wound. Already, the itch of healing swarmed around the puncture.

"Mom!" shrieked Tammy. She focused on him with an intense look of concentration.

The Red Rider flinched and emitted a wail of confused agony, appearing bewildered.

"The heck did you do?" rasped Allison.

"Flooding his mind with Justin Bieber music."

I took the opportunity to attack, scoring a nice slash down his chest, bloodying his armor. He recovered in time to deflect my follow up. I pressed the advantage, but our blades crossed five times without finding flesh again. When I raised my arm to swing again, he stomp kicked me in the chest.

That knocked me away enough for him to break and run for the doors. As he passed, I spun with vampiric speed, slicing a deep wound into the back of his left thigh. The *crack* of the blade striking his femur rattled my knuckles.

Flaming black blood sprayed on the floor. He staggered down to one knee but kept dragging himself forward. Tammy stared at him with a constipated expression. Boy band music appeared to have lost its ability to distract him again.

A magic bolt from Allison nailed the Red Rider in the chest, knocking him over sideways barely a second before the horse rammed into her, throwing her to the floor into a slide. It went to trample her, but Anthony bowled into it, knocking the beast on its side.

Kingsley, a streak of black fur, dashed by from the left and pounced on the Rider again. The two whirled in circles, too fast for me to have any clear opening to strike. They spun around and around in a tornado of punches, snapping jaws, and werewolf claws.

A loud roar from the left accompanied a blast of orange light.

The horse bathed Anthony in a huge gout of fire. Though he cringed, he appeared unfazed. Hmm. Guess that horse isn't too bright. Trying to burn the Fire Warrior… Still, something tells me I really don't want to get hit by that blast. Vampires and fire don't get along. The Red Rider eventually stabbed Kingsley in a tender spot, causing the big guy to involuntarily transform back to his human self. In a display of speed and strength that made me appreciate Kingsley all over again, the hairy oaf hurled the Rider across the room.

A weary Allison picked herself up off the floor, rubbing her left shoulder.

Kingsley swooned to one knee, cradling his groin. He bled from a slice on the inside of his thigh, a hand's width short of ground zero... and he looked quite pissed off.

Allie! Down! shouted Tammy in our heads.

The Red Rider pulled his crossbow and shot at Allison at the same instant she hurled herself flat to the floor. His quarrel passed over her and hit the wall, blackening the stone with a splat of decay. Another quarrel appeared in the weapon and he aimed at Tammy—who stood there like a deer in the headlights.

"Tammy!" I shouted, throwing myself forward, reaching for the projectile.

I snatched the quarrel out of midair, but the instant my fingers closed around it, a flailing, flying, warhorse crashed into me. We spun head over heels a few times and landed in a heap. Evid-ently, Anthony had similar ideas about protecting his sister and had thrown the horse to block the quarrel.

"Get off me you ugly piece of shit." I shoved at the beast, which also appeared to be attempting to right itself.

Somewhere, Tammy screamed. Allison let off an angry shriek. Something exploded, shaking the floor and making the iron chandeliers above us rattle. The horse finally floated up and off me, surrounded by glowing yellow light. Allison made an 'away with you' gesture, and the beast rocketed like a missile into the altar, cracking it.

A smoldering Red Rider charged at Allison, seeming more intent to attack her with his teeth than his blade. Any magic he could glean from her would make him even more powerful. We truly had caught the bastard at his weakest. A fabulous stroke of luck? Perhaps.

Meanwhile, the Rider brushed off the pelting of magical bolts she hurled at him, walking straight into the barrage and backing her against the door. Kingsley rolled around on the floor, struggling to remove a crossbow quarrel from his left pectoral. My little Tammy leapt *at* the Red Rider—stopping my heart—in an effort to shove him away from Allison, but he knocked her over on her ass with little effort.

It did *not* make me feel confident to see the horrible wound I'd slashed into his leg already gone. Damn. So much for a walk in the park.

I sprinted after him. Evidently, he sensed my blade coming and spun to defend. In this place, he fought with much greater strength and speed, fending off my strikes, no longer physically weaker than me. Against my better instincts, I listened to

Elizabeth's advice and let myself get angrier, thinking of that poor girl sitting on the fountain outside, how she didn't deserve to die the way she did. How none of those innocent girls—my prior incarnation included—deserved their fates.

My arms burned from the effort of overexerting myself. The ringing of our blades grew louder. Swing by swing, I forced him to back off. Every so often, I moved just fast enough to slip in under his defenses and rip long gashes in his chest.

"Mommy!" shouted Tammy, sounding terrified.

I disengaged with a flap of my wings, leaping up and hovering high near the ceiling so I could keep the Red Rider in view while glancing back over my shoulder at my daughter.

She flailed around on the floor, having ceased existing from the knees down. Allison, too, showed signs of fading away, her entire left arm missing. I glanced down at myself and noticed I'd pretty much gone fully transparent.

Shit. Not good.

Our timer's about done.

"Come on, Vincent. Please… just a little more time."

Tammy's legs faded back in.

"Thank you," I whispered.

The Red Rider sprinted for the doors, but bounced off them with an echoing *boom,* triggering a wave of glow that swept around the walls in the luminous writing Allison made. He rammed himself at the barrier again, but it held.

"Looks like you can't just poof here," I said, before diving down into an aerial strike.

I set upon him with enough speed that even he couldn't defend from my first swing. The Devil Killer opened a rent in his back that easily breached his left lung and sliced every rib on that side. It barely slowed him down. He spun with an elbow smash that hit me in the head, knocking me into the wall.

And glared at Allison.

Crap. He knew he couldn't get out of here as long as she remained alive. If she died, her magic would fade, and he'd slip away. But... he's not slowing down. What the hell? This sword is supposed to be able to kill *anything*.

Mom! shouted Tammy in my mind. *His crown! He's afraid you'll damage it. That's gotta be important. Break it!*

I sensed Elizabeth gathering strength. It didn't feel as though she intended to try overpowering me for control, but her stirring raised my defenses.

Sssamantha. It is time to send all the magic he stole from those helpless innocents back where it belongs. This creature is a wretch even by my standards. You want to avenge those children, don't you? You want the magic he stole to go back where it belongs, do you not?

Yeah... Wait. Back? He hasn't consumed it?

He has, but he holds it inside. When you destroy

him, it will be free to return where it came from. Unlike you, those children *reincarnate. The defenseless little girls he murdered will be reborn. When they do, you want them to have their magic back, don't you?*

I snarled to myself. I *did* want them to get their magic back, but I also wanted mine back, too, dammit. Sure, I knew that would never happen, but impossibility didn't stop people from *wanting* stuff. Orphans want their parents back, but it could never happen.

Focus on your want for the magic to go back where it belongs when you strike him down, said Elizabeth.

The Red Rider pounced at Allison. She screamed and leapt to the side, firing off a magical bolt with both hands. It set off an explosion that knocked them both flat on their backs and sliding. Allison didn't get up, though she continued to breathe at least. Kingsley staggered over, the crossbow bolt missing from his chest. He went to grab the Red Rider, but his hands had vanished.

"Dammit," muttered Kingsley, then transformed in an instant, clamping his teeth down on the Rider's shoulder, his pawless forelegs waving at the air.

I let off a scream from the deepest, angriest recesses of all my revulsion at everything the Red Rider did to the innocent, to my former self, even to J.C. Such torment that man had suffered for centuries at the loss of his little girl… and leapt into the air. Kingsley, fangs still sunk in the man's shoulder, angled his eyes upward at me. He held the Red Rider in place as I dove from the crest of a fifteen-foot high arc.

Wings spread wide, I chopped the Devil Killer down in a two-handed grip.

The blade struck the top of his head, cleaving the skull to the middle of his neck.

Two halves of a thin, brass crown fell away, sputtering magical energy from the cut points. The broken artifact released a blast of energy that launched Kingsley away and sent him sliding. A loud whinnying roar came from the right along with a loud *crack*. I shot a brief glance at the Fire Warrior twisting the horse's head around in a way no spine was ever meant to bend. I don't know what horrified me more: seeing a creature that resembled a horse being twisted like that, or that my son did it.

I turned my attention once more to the Red Rider, who stood in a swooning posture, his head still split in half straight down the middle. Full of sorrow and anger for all the evil he perpetrated, I raised the Devil Killer and wanted more than anything for his evil to end and all the magic he stole from all those innocents to go back where it belonged.

Roaring, I hurled my strength into a sideways slash that cut clean through his neck, then spun with the attack and stabbed the sword to the hilt in his chest. I ripped it clear and hacked down again, almost cutting him from neck to crotch.

"You are *such* a dork." Tammy sighed.

"What?" I asked.

"Anthony's thinking 'Samantha Moon wins… triple combo.'"

The Fire Warrior grinned.

"I don't get it," I muttered.

"*Mortal Kombat,* Mom." Tammy sighed. "It's a video game."

Meanwhile, a swarm of white-robed girls streamed into the room, the patter of bare feet on stone floor almost deafening. Gone were their emotionless expressions, replaced with natural smiles and gasps of "where am I" or "what happened?" as well as dozens of remarks in not-English. An incredible sense of relief and joy emanated from them. I even caught sight of one who looked like Daisy.

Oh my God; she was so damn young.

I couldn't help but snarl, and stabbed the Devil Killer into the Red Rider's heart once more.

The body finally flopped to the side, glowed orange, and exploded in a wave of brilliant white-yellow light.

Yeah. I should've seen that coming.

I barely had time to think 'this is going to hurt' before the energy blast tossed me flying backward into a white void.

Screaming…

20.

I can't say I've often wondered what it would feel like to be a victim of the electric chair.

Though, I think I have a relatively decent idea now. Along with a physical impact of a speeding city bus running into me, the most bizarre energy I've ever experienced rippled through me, like being microwaved, electrocuted, and exposed to the sun all at once… along with an overdose of cocaine.

A seeming eternity later, the overwhelming charge faded enough for me to perceive upward flight. And not just flight... but a rocket launch. Gradually, I slowed from squirrel that stepped on a land mine speed to jet plane to peregrine falcon to thrown baseball. When I collected myself enough to control a hover, I realized the explosion that launched me had been so powerful it not only blasted me straight out of my clothes, it replaced them with a white robe like the ones those girls had been wearing.

As far as I could see in every direction lay clouds—that is, as the floor beneath me. Bright sunlight bathed me from above, though rather than dread and fear, it brought a powerful sense of love and safety. So strong was the radiance that even when I realized I must have met my final death from what-ever force the Red Rider exploded with, and I would never see my children again, I didn't even feel like crying. As much as I knew I should be devastated—not to mention worried that they, too, may have been killed—I lacked the ability to feel anything but contentment.

"Sam," said a familiar voice.

I turned.

J.C.—my once-father, not the other J.C.—stepped out of a bank of mist. Though he appeared quite elderly, and even a bit on the frail side, he walked with strength unbefitting his age. He, too, wore a similar white robe and approached me with open arms.

"Am I… dead?"

My once-father embraced me with the fervor of a parent who hadn't seen their child in centuries. "Yes, Samantha."

I closed my eyes and cringed, silently saying farewell to Tammy, Anthony, Allison, and Kingsley.

"But not in the way you think," said Jeffcock.

"Er, what?" I pulled back.

He smiled a paternal, loving smile that chased away much of my anxiety. "You're a vampire, Sam. You're already dead."

"But didn't I blow myself apart when I killed the Red Rider?"

J.C. shook his head. "No... but most of the magic he stole did pass through you on its way back to the third dimension. It hurtled you up through the frequencies."

"Like a squirrel on a land mine."

He grinned. "Perhaps you had some help there."

"Wait. Rand killed you. How can you be here? Are you the Van Gogh version?"

"I am me, Sam. And yes, the hunter destroyed me. I am to return to the Origin, but have been allowed to wait here to see you one final time. When we part, I shall be reabsorbed into creation." He embraced me. "It is so, so good to be able to hold you again."

"I'm sorry."

"You don't need to apologize."

"I mean, for... I dunno. I'm sorry you never tried talking to me, or if I did anything that kept you away."

"None of what happened to me is in any way your fault. I made my choices and kept my distance. The only error was underestimating Rand. I asked you not to pick up my mantle and pursue the

Rider." He winked. "But I am glad you did. I can return to creation with no regrets but that I was not allowed to live a full life with my daughter beside me."

"Too young." I looked down. "I'm going to randomly think about her and get all sad and maudlin for years."

"Don't." Jeffcock wiped my cheek as if I were crying, though I couldn't weep here. "My daughter has been reincarnated into you, and when your time does eventually come, you shall also return to the Origin. In some way, I know we will be reunited again."

No matter how sad I became, I felt like a child cradled in their parents' lap, assured everything would be okay... a child young enough to believe their parent could fix any problem in the world merely by wanting to.

"Easier said than accepted." I squeezed my fingers into his shoulders, not wanting to let go, despite knowing the pervasive sense of security didn't come from him. "Are we..."

"On the 99th dimension. I'm waiting at the Origin's doorstep, so to speak. I have only one place left to go now."

I bowed my head.

"Sam, listen to me." J.C. lifted my chin with a gentle finger, making me look him in the eye. "You are about to experience a tremendous change. You are a force of creation, too."

"I think I'm more a force of destruction."

He chuckled. "No, Sam. You are a creator—of sorts."

"Of sorts? I'm about as creative as a rock. I never even liked coloring books as a kid. The most creative thing I ever did was come up with ways to break into the farm down the road to grab stuff, or steal food from the supermarket without getting caught… until I got too old to get away with that stuff. It's not 'cute' to steal food after like twelve."

"You *are* a force of creation, but no Van Gogh, true. Not like Charlie Reid who created the world of Dur. No, you don't invent new worlds or shape alternate realities. But you do alter the fabric of your world, the third dimension. Only… slowly."

"I really think you're being given some bad information. If I could shape reality, so many things would be so different."

J.C. grasped my hand in both of his. "You do shape your reality, but it is quite gradual. That which you truly want, the Universe will accommodate. I'm not entirely sure when this happened, though I suspect it is a result of a confluence of certain unique characteristics. Your alchemical bloodline, the hereditary witchcraft, the power you have obtained becoming an immortal, even your death at the hands of the Red Rider five centuries ago. Somewhere amid all of that coming to exist in the same individual, it caused a once-in-a-millennia circumstance. Perhaps this is how you were able to defeat the Red Rider."

"Speaking of..." I glanced off at the clouds, then up at the endless perfect blue sky. Traces of orange and amber shimmered at the horizon, an unearthly light more beautiful than anything my wildest imagination could've conjured up. "What happened to all those girls?"

"The beings you saw there were not souls, mere shadows of the energy he stole. That energy has returned to the third dimension." J.C. brushed a hand at my cheek. "I didn't ask you to take up my quest, but I am without words to express how grateful I am that you have put that monster to rest." He paused. "I have missed you so much, little one."

I opened my mouth to speak, but no words came out. Just a small, choking gasp.

He smiled and held out his arms, and I found myself veritably throwing myself into them. As I did, he pulled me into a tight embrace and never had I felt such love... and I doubted I would ever feel such love again... from anyone, ever. I hugged him back with all my heart, not entirely sure if I should consider him my father, my sire, both, or something different. After a moment, I realized I no longer held on to another person's body. When I opened my eyes, J.C. had vanished, save for a fleeting white glow racing upward into the sky.

"Goodbye..." I whispered.

I kept staring at the distancing smear of light until it faded away.

The magnitude of gazing up at the hundredth dimension—the Origin—hit me. Part of me wondered if I should bow my head, kneel, or show some sort of reverence. Another part grew curious and wondered if my wings could carry me up one more dimension.

Strong benevolence fell upon me from the sky, along with a sense that a tremendously powerful force knew I tried to see it. For no reason I could explain, the idea that it was not my time to go there washed over me. I'd been brought to the 99th for a last farewell with a man who loved me across centuries and lifetimes. The Origin, vast as it was, had noticed the last wish of one seemingly insignificant person, and granted it. He, she, or it had allowed us to have that moment. It had spoken to me without words. Humbled, I bowed my head, too aware that I needed to return home.

"I understand."

As if a trapdoor under my feet swung open, I plummeted straight down, though I didn't scream… or even feel a sense of alarm.

21.

Placid white light surrounded me for only a few seconds before fading.

The sense of falling gave way to standing on solid ground with no transition, no impact, not even a feeling of slowing. I found myself in the courtyard of the Red Rider's sixth-dimensional castle, surrounded by hundreds of empty white robes. My clothing had returned to normal, which made me wonder if I had only ascended in spirit... like an astral projection.

I looked around, calling out for Tammy, Anthony, Kingsley, or Allison, but none of them replied to my voice echoing into the halls of this abandoned place. As I took a step toward the door, wondering if they perhaps remained in the cathedral chamber, waiting for me, a tremendous searing pain lanced through my heart.

Sweet mama. It hurt *so* damn bad I nearly blacked out.

Clutching my chest, I fell to my knees, paralyzed.

The horrible pain faded after an agonizing moment, shifting down into my stomach and manifesting as nausea. It had been years since I felt sick like that, worse than even my first few days as a vampire trying to eat solid food. A convulsion shook my body. Once, again, and a third time hard enough to knock me flat on my front.

I retched, and a torrent of foul, black ichor blasted out of my mouth, streaming from my nostrils as well. The flow of liquid gushing up my throat gathered solidity, becoming a gummy mass as big as my forearm. Puking became gagging. I no longer vomited, rather twitched there helpless on the ground as *something* crawled out of me.

My face against the cold stone floor, I stared across the black puddle at the front end of the serpentine mass. It sprouted arms, dragging itself forward. A head formed, the arms thickening to human proportion. Still, I retched. Hell, my jaw threatened to crack from the girth of the fleshy slug creeping inch by inch out from inside me.

Another flash of blinding pain hit me in the face and jaw. If not for being a vampire, I probably would have fainted. So much for my ability to alter reality. If I wanted anything in that moment, it would've been unconsciousness—assuming I couldn't simply make it all stop.

The slug shrank in diameter, and another several feet of horror only as thick as a garden hose pulled out of my throat. It joined the writhing mass on the stones a short distance from me, curling and unwinding. My throat finally clear, I choked on slime, puked bile, and proceeded to cough and gag for a minute or two.

When I looked up again, the thing I'd… given birth to had lightened from jet black to a medium brown, to a pale fleshy color and had taken on the sultry shape of an incredibly beautiful woman. Naked as a newborn babe, she lay curled up in a patch of horrid ebony ooze. Dark hair fanned out on the stone behind her. She shook off the disorientation of her coming to be, and rose to her feet. Despite her nakedness, the woman exuded an air of authority and absolute confidence.

Still fighting the urge to gag, I fought my way up on to my knees so I could stand.

"Hello, Samantha," said the woman—in Elizabeth's voice, minus the serpentine hiss. A faint accent, perhaps Egyptian or something of that sort replaced it. "I appreciate that you know you should be kneeling before me."

I gawked, too stunned to even finish standing out of spite. "What?"

She threw her head back and emitted a haughty laugh, then gestured at one of the white robes. It leapt into the air as if alive and wrapped itself around her. "You performed beyond my expectations, dear girl."

It finally hit me that I really didn't want to be kneeling in front of this bitch, so I scrambled to my feet. My stomach felt like I'd been used as a heavy bag by twenty MMA fighters. "How… What's…" I reached deep inside my head for Elizabeth's dark presence. It had been so damn long since my mind belonged solely to me, I almost didn't recognize that she'd gone. Nothing answered my inner thoughts but silence.

"Do not burden yourself with the details, dear. You played your part perfectly. And as a token of my appreciation, I will not destroy you." She stepped closer, a dark smile parting her full lips. "However, should you act against me in the future, I will not hesitate to put you down."

"I'm dreaming." I backed away from her. "You're not really there. That blast knocked me out and I'm dreaming."

"You don't dream, Samantha. Remember?"

I stopped. "So what the hell is this?"

"Reality. The sixth dimension. You ought to be on your way before that poor painter works himself to death keeping you intact."

I could only stare at her.

"Oh, the confusion on your face is priceless. I should ask him to paint you just like that." She laughed. "You really believed I wanted you to kill the Devil so the other dark masters and I could escape the void and not fear being chased down?"

"Yeah, that was kind of what I thought." I glanced at the sword in my hand. "I mean, what else is a girl supposed to do with the Devil Killer but kill the Devil?"

She clucked her tongue at me. "I cannot fault you for believing what I wanted you to believe, dear girl. I created a plan, and you executed it perfectly, not even aware you did exactly as I intended. All the while, you thought you worked against me, contained me…"

"I think you're full of shit."

"Your role in all this, Samantha Moon, was never to kill the Devil. You cannot kill something like that, an entity the entire world—or most of it—believes in. The Universe will simply replace it with another to fill the role. From the moment you were born into this life, I set you on a path to fulfill a specific purpose. And you have done so. Did you not think it odd that you suddenly found yourself missing your magic like some child whose puppy had been stolen? Don't tell me you can't believe the most powerful telepath ever to set foot on the Earth couldn't manipulate a mind she inhabited without you noticing the subtle nudges."

I blinked.

She laughed.

"Okay…" I pointed at her. "If you weren't trying to free your dark masters from the threat of the Devil, what the hell are you talking about?"

She twirled a lock of black hair around her finger. "All the magic that filthy creature had siphoned up has returned to the world. Magic, Samantha. And that power is *mine.* The void no longer contains us. We no longer have any need to fear the Devil. He should fear me."

Oh, this bitch has gone full megalomaniac. "I still think I'm somehow hallucinating or dreaming. I'm containing you, stopping you from wreaking havoc."

Elizabeth laughed again. "Oh, Samantha. No one uses 'wreaking havoc' outside of bad movies. But this is very much real, my dear girl. You had contained me, or so you thought. But a prisoner who is happy in her cell is no prisoner. I was right where I needed to be—influencing you. Jeffcock had it correct. You have acquired some aspects of a creator. That exposure to Dur, the painter, your wonderfully intricate combination of bloodlines. You accepted the 'burden' you thought you carried of containing me, but all along you wanted to be free of it."

"I had no choice. I gave up normality to contain you for the greater good."

"Ahh yes, but you resented that. You wanted to be free of me. Admit it, Samantha. You wouldn't have let me out, but you also wished for an escape from the responsibility."

I stared down, unsure if she tried to trick me

again or if that little sliver of doubt gnawing on the back of my mind meant she spoke truth.

"I wanted you to resent me. I wanted you to desire *your* freedom. That you would acquire the ability to influence reality was something I foresaw before you were even born into this life. You destroyed the Red Rider at long last. You are the only creature capable of doing what you just did… a former witch from an alchemical bloodline, an immortal, with nascent trace of creator ability."

"Are you seriously trying to tell me the Red Rider was more important or powerful than the Devil?" I blinked in shock. "Seriously?"

"More important to *me*, yes. More powerful, well that depends on your definition of power. Only a handful of people knew of him, and none of them continue to believe he exists, so his destruction is permanent. Unlike the Devil who is feared, reviled, and even worshiped by vast numbers of people. The Rider murdered innocents. He murdered you in a prior life."

I folded my arms. Despite every bit of me wanting to accuse her of lying, I couldn't. For an instant, I considered lashing out at her, but hesitated. Something was wrong here. My body ached, and I felt as worn out as a spent battery. My arms and legs cooperated only under protest, like I'd way overexerted myself at the gym and needed a full day to lie in bed and do nothing. That, and I couldn't shake the sense of wonder and doubt triggered by

J.C.'s comment to me that I was about to change. Well, Elizabeth somehow leaving my body and growing a new one certainly counted as *change.* But, what did that mean for me? Had I become human again? If so, attacking this bitch would be a huge mistake.

She laughed. "It would be a huge mistake for you regardless, dear. And no. You're not human again, quaint and romantic as that idea is."

"So..." I rubbed my stomach, which *still* ached. "What exactly happened?"

"Thank you, Samantha, for being a good little part of my plan. Fret not, my dear. You have taken your revenge, and you have given me what I wanted the most." Elizabeth patted me on the cheek. "The world."

I opened my mouth, but before a word could form in my brain, she patted me again.

Her palm touched my face with a crash like a thunderclap, knocking my surroundings into a spinning blur. Again, I felt as though I plummeted straight down past the ground and kept right on going, though by no means as gracefully or gently as my descent from the Origin's doorstep.

No, this time, I fell like a damn rock.

22.

I'm not sure at what point the disorienting spin-fall stopped and I found myself gazing up at a blue sky dotted with fuzzy white clouds.

One moment, I'm hurtling downward, tumbling over and over, too weak and out of it to even scream... the next I'm flat on my back. Well, at least my landing didn't hurt. Or maybe I'm in so much pain from everything else, a high-speed collision with the ground didn't even register on the ouch-o-meter.

Grass fluttering in a calm breeze tickled my cheek. Somewhere, birds chirped. The sun hung high in the sky, noon or close to it. An instant of panic started deep in my soul at being caught outside on such a bright day, but then I remembered my rings. I heaved a sigh of relief and raised my hands to smile at them—and stared in confusion.

No, the rings remained. That's not what caused my brain to seize up.

My fingernails no longer looked grotesquely pointed. I lay there in the grass for a long few minutes, simply staring at my hands, at nails that looked exactly as they had for my entire life prior to that fateful night in Hillcrest Park.

Ooo-kay. That's bizarre.

I concentrated on trying to extend my claws, but nothing sprouted from my fingertips. Umm... All right. I know I hated my fangs. I've tried as much as I can not to even think about them ever since I scared the crap out of some little girl years ago. Except for that time I got stuck in 1862 and had no choice but to feed from live cows, I'd largely almost forgotten I even *had* fangs. But, yeah. Vampire. The universe creates what people believe in, and people believe vampires and fangs are like pizza and pepperoni.

"Okay. This is for scientific purposes only."

I braced my jaw and tried to extend my fangs... and felt like an idiot doing some kind of yogic eardrum-popping exercise. When that didn't accomplish anything, I reached into my mouth and felt around at my canines. Even retracted, they'd been sharp enough to punch holes in thin metal sheets... but they felt normal now.

"Oh, this is too damn weird. What happened to me?"

Elizabeth? Are you there? I mentally lifted the rock off the oubliette lid, then pulled the lid open, searching for her. Only, it felt like the mental prison pit I kept her in had been filled up with dirt. No Elizabeth.

Gone.

My brain belonged to me and me alone.

I curled up in a ball and wept. How long I'd wanted to be free of her... It seemed too good to be true. But, really... it wasn't good. Not at all. I had contained her specifically to protect the world. I accepted that role, but the bitch had a point. I really did resent having to be the one stuck with that job. But what if she hadn't lied to me? If it had been her plan all along for me to do everything I did, with the climax of destroying the Red Rider... then it had never really been my destiny to 'contain' her. She only made everyone believe that. She'd made *me* believe that.

Or maybe it had been my destiny and I screwed it up. I let her talk to me. I listened.

Am I still a vampire?

I stared at the sun protection ring. Okay, a few seconds won't kill me. It'll hurt like a bastard, but it won't kill me. I had to know. Hell, my claws were gone.

I hadn't shaken like that since I'd been a little kid dreading what Dad would do to me when he got home. Okay, so I almost accidentally burned down the house, but I didn't mean to. And hey, Dad didn't even hit me. He wasn't a violent guy. Violence took energy. Dad weaponized guilt. Talked at me for like an hour about how sad everyone would be if we lost our house.

Hey, it worked... I never did try 'chemistry experiments' with matches again.

Trembling, I grabbed the sun ring and eased it off my finger, braced for horrible pain.

The ring slipped free... and I felt no different. The sun warmed my face and hands, no burn. No pain. Not even discomfort. I swear I giggled like a six-year-old girl getting a pony for her birthday. Overcome by happiness, I leapt to my feet and danced around in circles for a little while.

My claws were gone... and maybe I'd miss them. They did come in handy. Fangs are gone, good riddance. Those things always bugged me. Such an inhuman reminder of being a monster. Wait a second... what's that noise?

Thump. Thump. Thump.

Heartbeat... coming from... me?

My head spun.

More testing. I spun in place, gazing out over miles of endless meadow. It didn't appear oil painted, nor did it look hyper-real, so I felt certain I'd fallen back into the third dimension. Exactly *where* I was, I couldn't say. This field could've been in like Oklahoma as easily as Germany. Still, no one was around to see me. Did I still have a link to Talos?

I stripped naked. For a few seconds, the distraction of basking in the sun occupied me. Years ago, I'd been a beach bum. I never did the nudist beach thing; however, I'm a little short on bikinis at the moment. Basking in the sun, not having any fear of it almost brought me to tears. On a lark, I picked up a potato-sized rock and hurled it as hard as I could throw. It zoomed off as if fired from a cannon. Right. I remained much stronger than a human should be, about the same as I'd been as a vampire. Time for another test: I called out to Talos. The single flame appeared in my mind, dancing against a field of blackness. I felt myself moving toward it... rapidly.

The transformation, as always, was instant. I unfurled Talos's great wings, stretched his long neck to look back the scaled, heavily muscled body.

Well, I was definitely *not* a normal human again. Though, I dare say I might not be undead anymore. I seemed to have a heartbeat and my hands, at least, didn't look as pale as they should be. Or were. Not *should* be. I shouldn't have been pale, that had been a side effect of undeath. They looked like *me* again.

Son of a bitch.

It occurred to me that the image of me I'd once seen in Max's book with wings, before I'd met the Angel of Death, had been rather lifelike. Not pale and ghoulish like I'd been. Holy crap. My great dragon like head spun.

Talos, what the heck happened to me?

Hmm... I sense a great deal of... magic inside you now. It was not there before. It is powerful, but raw, untrained. I believe you may have absorbed some of the power that blasted away from the Red Rider when it returned to the third dimension. Perhaps that which he stole from your prior incarnation is once again yours.

Hmm. Elizabeth admitted to prodding me to miss my magic like a stolen puppy. But why would she do that? Oh, shit... If I really did have some scrap of creator power, how much of reality had I shaped?

Your incarnation this time was due for a peak in power. Fate has strange ways of ensuring it comes to pass. I believe you may have gotten your wish.

Am I a vampire? Elizabeth is gone. She's not in here anymore. She... somehow made a new body for herself.

I cannot say for sure, but you no longer appear to be undead. You are no mortal, Samantha. Your soul remains fully contained within your body, still apart from the cycle. When your time finally ends, you will return to the Origin.

J.C. said I'm a creator. But I can't believe that.

His smile stretched across the back of my consciousness. *You wanted to fly, and you reincarnated as a dragon in a prior life. You continued wanting to fly, and here I am, happy to lend you my body in your world. You felt jealous of Annie and her relationship to the fairies, wanting your magic back... and here it is. You resented having to contain Elizabeth, and she is now gone. You may be a form of creator, but you don't make whole worlds in hours.*

She said I have a slow effect on *this* world. And, Elizabeth made me want my magic. Did I really want it or was that her mind-controlling me?

Talos seemed to think that over, or maybe peered into my head. *I believe you convinced yourself that you had lost all hope of being the witch you were born to be in this lifetime. A part of you did desire it again, as she says. Elizabeth may have only brought the desire to the surface... while removing your barrier of grief and acceptance of loss.*

I can't grieve what I never knew. I sighed out the great dragon's nostrils.

Well, you did see a fairy when you were nine, Sam. One does not have to be an adult for the cynicism of the world to cloud young eyes.

I felt like Kingsley during a discussion of higher dimensions.

Say again?

Talos chuckled. *In simpler terms, your impoverished childhood placed the burden of maturity on you at a younger age. Your mind closed to the magic around you far younger than most.*

So what the hell am I if I'm not an undead vampire anymore?

No idea. I am merely a dragon, not an Oracle. Perhaps your alchemist friend may offer some insight.

The exertion of the past hour or so finally caught up with me, and a strong pang of hunger gripped my gut. It felt pretty much the same as the few times I screwed up and went too long without a blood meal, but ever so slightly different. The light-headedness and fatigue were new. I started to think about finding some pig blood, but the mere idea of drinking that mess brought me to the edge of vomiting again, so sick that I lapsed out of Talos form and fell on all fours, naked as a fairy in the grass.

The last time I threw up, I resurrected a source of ultimate evil. Not in a hurry to do that again. I clamped both hands over my mouth and tried to stop thinking about blood with little nuggets of pig flesh floating in it.

Oh, this is way too weird.

23.

Well, I've found myself in stranger circumstances than this before—though not by much.

At least Talos remained connected to me. Why I found that a relief, I couldn't quite say. I'd have been lying if I said I didn't often miss being a normal human, though I needed to qualify that.

I plopped down in the grass and put my clothes back on, happy the 'Talos test' worked. Yeah, sure, for the first couple of months after my attack in Hillcrest Park, I tried to disbelieve what happened, begged the universe for a do-over, that sort of thing. But, honestly, I wasn't so much opposed to being a vampire as I was to losing my family and the life I'd worked so hard for. My job at HUD, my husband, my kids… I once feared I'd lose all of it. And, well, I did lose everything except my kids. And I did kind of lose them in a way after all; they're far different than they would've been normally.

Of course, Anthony would've been dead at seven otherwise. Yeah, maybe I would still have Danny in my life if I never became a vampire, but I'd have lost my son. That's a trade I couldn't make. Now I have another loss to worry about. Tammy, powerful as she is, was on a collision course with insanity or worse, suicide. Fortunately, a distinct difference existed between those who wanted to end their lives due to mental illness, and those who reached that point due to things like chronic pain—or in Tammy's case—unending voices in her head. In those cases, the person didn't want to die as much as they needed to stop the source of their pain.

I also considered the possibility that with Elizabeth now gone, the source of Tammy's telepathic prowess was also gone; meaning, perhaps Tammy's abilities would wane. Perhaps. But I suspected that her gifts had stuck, so to speak. Although awakened by the proximity of Elizabeth and enhanced by the demoness within, Tammy's latent abilities had come through.

Still, fingers crossed that I would return home to find a daughter who would report a diminishing of telepathic power.

That is, of course, if all was well with them. In truth, I didn't know where I'd landed or if my kids—and Kingsley and Allison—were okay. First things first... find out where the hell I was.

I stood, finished getting dressed, and looked around again at the pastoral field. Being outside in broad daylight without wearing my ring tweaked a nerve of dread, but I couldn't argue that I wasn't on fire—or even uncomfortable. I'd spent so long defying the sun with the medallion and rings that it didn't feel *too* weird.

Which brought up another issue. I presently felt hungrier than I could ever remember being. Wait, no. I hit this point once before in the past—and wound up attacking a creep at a parking garage in the midst of a blind frenzy. If I remained a vampire, and I didn't even have fangs, how the hell was I supposed to feed?

Again, the mere thought of consuming blood made me sick to my stomach. I stopped thinking about it before remembering the way those little nuggets of pig gristle or skin felt going down my throat.

Why did such a normal reaction of disgust to that feel so bizarre?

Ugh.

Time to go home.

I closed my eyes, thought of home, and called the dancing flame, but only a faint spark appeared along with a withering pang of hunger that nearly put me on my knees. Dammit! Seriously? I can't teleport anymore? That's like taking the car keys away from an eighteen-year-old after she *just* got her license. My panic ebbed in a few seconds along with the wracking pain clawing at my guts.

Wait, no. The flame *tried* to appear. I was just too damn weak to do it. It hadn't been *that* long since I fed, but as best I could figure, trying to hold myself together in higher dimensions took a lot out of me. Or maybe Elizabeth drained me to make herself a new body. And I also had an entire dimension's worth of magical energy explode through me when the Red Rider died.

So, yeah, that could explain why I felt like a wrung out dish towel.

Guess I'm walking.

Wait…

I thought about the wings the Angel of Death gave me—and they sprouted into existence, unfurling into their feathered magnificence with a barely audible *whuff*—and a twinge of mild pain that reminded me I ran on empty. Every little supernatural thing I did hurt. No slight on Talos, but I love the way these wings don't require I strip. Somehow, they phased right through my clothes, which made them quite a bit stealthier. Much easier to recover from a quick landing when I don't have to explain why I look like I made a wrong turn at the nudist colony. Sad thing is, the area I grew up in back in California… people probably wouldn't even notice or care about the nakedness. Lot of hippies around there.

Anyway… I pulled out my phone hoping to get

some good news from the GPS app. It didn't disappoint. I'm still in Cali, near the Carrizo Plain National Monument. Nice. Not too far from home.

***

I flew at a medium altitude, low enough for my still-sharper-than-human eyes to see people on the ground, but too high for anyone to perceive me clearly. If anything, they'd probably mistake me for a California condor or something. You know, because most people wouldn't expect a woman with wings to be cruising around LA.

Soon after I glided in over Fullerton, I spotted my crew hovering around the Momvan in the driveway of my house. Though I couldn't hear them from this altitude and distance, their body language made me think they tried to figure out where to go to find me. I leaned into a dive, picking up speed, and headed straight for them.

Tammy sensed me coming first, and pointed up. Okay, so her power hadn't faded. Shit.

I swung my feet down and landed a bit harder than expected, on one knee with my fists against the driveway. I blamed the ungainly crash landing on fatigue and hunger. The instant my sneakers hit the pavement, a rush of energy hit me, like I'd started feeding on blood. Powerful blood too, like human blood.

And ugh. The idea of drinking blood seriously

disgusted me.

"Whoa," said Kingsley.

"Mom..." moaned Anthony in a tone he only used when genuinely sick or trying to fake his way out of school for the day.

"Gah!" Tammy grabbed her head. "Mom! Stop it!"

I lifted my head to look at them.

Kingsley swooned on his feet as if drunk. Anthony—back to his human form—leaned against the Momvan with an expression like he'd just finished running a marathon. Tammy scowled at me, though her mood radiated far more confusion than anger. Allison's eyes rolled back into her head and she stood there like a zombie.

Equally confused, I could only stare back at everyone... until I noticed faint white energy lines wisping out of their foreheads, which I inhaled like a desperate pothead trying to catch a secondary buzz off someone else's joint. My hunger ebbed from a freak out starvation level to 'damn I want a burger.'

"What the hell?" I asked no one in particular.

Allison snapped out of her mind fog and raised both hands at me in a gesture like a cop trying to stop traffic. A circle of white light drew itself in midair, as if a five-foot-wide pane of glass stuck to her palms. The wispy trails connecting everyone's heads to me vanished at once with a sensation like someone grabbed my blood bottle away from me before I'd finished eating.

"Sam... what the hell?" rasped Allison, a hint of anger in her voice.

"Sorry. I have no idea." I grabbed the Momvan and pulled myself up to stand. "Lot of weird shit just happened to me."

"Holy fuck!" shouted Tammy. "Elizabeth's gone!"

I pointed at her, ready to yell. Instead, I nodded weakly. "Ehh. You know what. I'm gonna let that f-bomb slide. This moment kinda deserves it."

Anthony folded his arms. "Can I bank one f-bomb for later use?"

I had more important things to care about than my kids swearing, so I halfheartedly nodded at him before hugging them both tight. Tammy swam around my thoughts, shivering at my memory of Elizabeth's conversation.

"What?" Allison ran over and stared into my eyes. "Oh, whoa. What the hell has happened to you, Sam? You like... have color in your cheeks."

"As soon as I figure it out, I'll let you all know." I pressed my face into Tammy's shoulder, squeezed her, then did the same with Anthony. He hugged me back with surprising strength, though it shouldn't have caught me off guard. He, too, had become something more than mortal.

"Sam, you were feeding on us," said Allison.

"What?" I let go of the hug to gawk at her. "But I didn't touch..."

"You were draining our *mental* energy. I think... you've. Hmm." Allison rubbed her chin. "You ever hear of a 'psychic vampire?'"

"Isn't that the dude at work that makes everyone tired just by being around them because he's so obnoxious?" asked Kingsley, chuckling.

"That's not the same thing." Allison grasped my face in both hands and stared into my eyes. "You've changed."

"Yeah. J.C. said I was going to..." I held up my hands, wiggling my fingers. "Check it out. No more manicurist nightmare."

"Mom! Where's your ring?" shouted Tammy. "You're gonna..." She blinked. "Not burn."

"Whoa," said Anthony.

Kingsley sniffed at me. "You're still an immortal. I don't see an aura. And I can't read your mind."

I nodded. "Do you still have a dark master lurking in there?" I asked, tapping his meaty chest. "Elizabeth said something about them exploding out of people..."

He nodded. "Yeah. Nothing's changed. He's still here."

"Mine's gone." I explained what happened with Elizabeth, something Tammy had already picked up on.

"It had to be because you were at like ground zero when the Red Rider went off like a Roman candle." Allison shivered.

"And what happened to you guys?" I swiped my

hair off my face and neatened it as best I could with my hands.

"Wanna go inside and sit or something?" asked Kingsley. "And we'll tell you."

I gazed up. "Actually... I want to enjoy the sun if you don't mind... at least for a moment."

"So, psychic vampire." Allison kept prodding me. "They feed on mental energy. In extreme cases, they can drain someone's psyche to the point they wind up PVS."

"Pretentious Vegan Syndrome?" asked Tammy.

Kingsley laughed, as did Anthony.

"No." Allison smirked. "Persistent vegetative state. They'd basically had their personalities and mental strength devoured."

"Eek." I blinked. "That's almost worse than draining someone's blood to the point of death."

"Well, the good news is, like with traditional vampires, you don't have to go that far. You could walk through a crowd and nip a little from everyone. They wouldn't notice and you'd be stuffed. You could do the same with animals. Anything living, really. Maybe even plants." Allison grinned. "This is actually pretty cool."

I couldn't help but look at her and think... *Elizabeth is gone, do I still need to be exiled from your head?*

Her eyes widened. "Oh, shit, Sam. You feel different..."

"Duh." I flared my eyebrows.

"No, I mean… you feel like a... baby witch."

My hands trembled as the realization of that dawned on me. I'd wanted my magic back. Had I seized on it when all that energy flowed through me on its way back to the third dimension? Or had my desire to send it all back where it belonged somehow restored it?

"You have a scent now, Sam." Kingsley sniffed at my neck—and couldn't help but kiss me. "And a pulse. And body heat." He looked at me like he couldn't wait to be alone together later.

"Lalalalalala," said Tammy, sticking her fingers in her ears. "Please stop thinking about Mom that way near me."

"I'm not undead anymore… but not human either."

"Werewolves and mermaids are immortal but not undead. Hmm. There is something else, too." He leaned back scratching his chin. "Maybe those angel wings are going deeper than we ever thought possible."

"Hah. Me? An angel? Don't be silly."

"Not an angel, perhaps just a trace of it." Allison walked around me.

"Okay, if that's true and I'm not an undead anymore and maybe like a quarter angel or whatever the fraction is… where'd the psychic vampire stuff come from?"

"Mom." Tammy stared into my eyes. "You never liked drinking blood. It always made you feel like a freak. But... you also spent so long as a vampire, you couldn't help but think of yourself that way. What if Talos was right about you having the ability to make stuff you want happen, just like real slow. Maybe you drink mental energy now because you thought of yourself as a vampire but hated the whole blood thing?"

Allison shrugged. "That makes about as much sense as anything else. The kid's got a good idea there. You'd gotten so used to being a vampire, some aspect of that is still present in whatever you've become now."

I ran my fingers through my hair, careful of my nails... okay, no longer worried about those sharp suckers. Score one for me. "So what happened to you guys? Were you really there? The fiend exploded and everything turned into white light."

"Yeah... you disappeared in a flash," said Kingsley. "A column of white light that shot straight up."

"Like the beams from *Ghostbusters*," added Anthony.

"More beams shot out from the corpse and hit the girls in robes. They all went from blank-faced mannequins to like actual people. But they only remained for a couple seconds each before their bodies disappeared and all the robes fell." Allison looked down, near to tears.

"Don't cry. They weren't real ghosts... magical echoes or something," I said.

"But they still represented all his victims." Allison sniffled.

"And they're all reincarnated. No point being sad about stuff we can't do anything to change. I got the son of a bitch, so at least no more innocent little witches will ever be... killed."

"Speaking of little witches," said Tammy in a bit of a sheepish tone. "I think you need to visit that big-ass tree by that kid's house again."

"Where'd that come from?" I asked.

"Her boyfriend called." Anthony grinned.

"Stuff it, Ant!" snapped Tammy, blushing, using a new nickname for her brother. Apparently, it was supposed to be ironic, considering Anthony could turn into something massive indeed.

Oh, yeah. She's definitely got a boyfriend.

Allison giggled, finding my daughter's embarrassment cute.

That aside, what possible connection could this theoretical boyfriend have to Annie the witch and her magical tree?

Tammy narrowed her eyes at me. *Not Annie or the tree. The fairies. They asked to see you. And, yeah. I wanna go, too.*

"Why don't we all go?" I asked with a smile.

"Huh?" Kingsley looked at me.

"We need to make a quick trip," I said, patting his cheek.

"Aren't you worn out and exhausted?" he asked.

"Yeah, but I feel better now. I'm *still* tired and

hungry, but you guys took the edge off. Sorry. I didn't even mean to absorb energy from you like that."

Allison put an arm around my shoulders. "It's okay. I know you didn't know you did it. But, we're going to need to work on your control."

"Just like learning how to feed for the first time…" I chuckled. "I've obviously got some ability to control it. Just need to work out the details."

"And that's beyond messed up." Tammy pointed at Kingsley. "You fed off another immortal. I didn't think vampires could do that?"

"I'm not your everyday vampire." I wagged my eyebrows.

24.

I parked the Momvan as near to the field as I could get without damaging any plant life.

We all hopped out and started the trek to the eucalyptus tree, no one much in the mood for more conversation. On the ride up here, we'd talked about Elizabeth being free—and alive again—though Kingsley thought she had become something else. Definitely not an ordinary human. Some kind of immortal with a fully-contained soul. Though, exactly what she was or what she could do, we could only guess... but one thing we all agreed on: it wouldn't be good.

Elizabeth had offered a truce with me out of some twisted sense of gratitude for doing her bidding and setting her loose upon the world. She also knew how to hurt me if she wanted to: harming my children. Though the woman promised to leave me alone if I didn't mess with her, and I damn sure knew if I pissed her off, she'd go straight for where it hurt me the most, I didn't fully trust her to actually leave me alone. Since her plan came to fruition and my destruction meant nothing to her anymore, the threat that I'd destroy myself with a sun bath if she ever hurt my children held no more weight.

Well, that and a sun bath wouldn't really bother me.

I spent the rest of the walk out to the tree having mixed thoughts about all the ways I tried to deal with the sun after becoming a vampire. Everything from when I still tried to keep my HUD job to that time I dropped Tammy off at school and nearly roasted myself in the parking lot.

My daughter's random blush told me she saw my memory of her going to preschool and how much I cried that day.

We found Annie sitting in the shade of the giant tree in a cute white sundress, a crown of pink flowers in her blonde hair, and a flower anklet on each leg. A dozen or more tiny people sat around her, some on her, others hovering nearby. Some wore skirts made of leaves, some merely glowed. All chattered merrily with the little girl, who looked so cute, happy, and normal I could almost forget what had happened to her.

Kingsley and Anthony hung back, my son being too 'macho' to go anywhere near fairies and the big werewolf not wanting to freak them out.

Annie looked up as I approached with Tammy and Allison beside me. Her smile turned into an expression of elation at seeing me.

"Hey there," I said.

"Hi." Annie waved. "Maple wanted to talk to you."

"Oooh," cooed Allison, gazing in awe at the fairies like she'd gone back to being twelve.

When Tammy *didn't* make fun of her, I glanced over. My kid appeared to be simultaneously thrilled at meeting a cloud of faeries as much as she tried to project ambivalence toward them. Miss Cool couldn't let anyone see her gushing inside. Yeah, okay, my kid had a goth streak, but she still evidently loved cute. And hey… fairies, right?

The fairies also glanced in my direction… and it hit me then that I saw them for what they were, not little balls of light. One glided up to me, the woman with the crown, Maple. I'm sure she'd been the one who allowed me a small glimpse of herself before, and had likely followed Annie back to the house when we returned.

Their queen, princess, or whatever, drifted up to my eye level on a trail of sparkling dust. I can't say I'd ever seen anyone give off so much happiness, except maybe Annie's parents. Though, this fairy appeared even happier than them. Probably because she knew exactly what the Red Rider would have done to Annie. Her parents had only thought killing her would've been the worst part. Little did they know….

I got the feeling Maple had pseudo-adopted Annie. Maybe witches have familiars or something and this kid won the lottery to get a fairy willing to be her companion. I had a fascination with owls. In fact, there'd been one that hung around my childhood home that I swore liked me, but I hadn't seen him since I went off to college.

The way Maple looked at me gave me the feeling she wanted to reward me for helping Annie. Before I could even think to tell her she didn't have to, that I would've busted my ass to save any innocent in that situation, she nodded at me as if in response to something, then glided over to Tammy, who dropped her too cool for school affect and let the little woman land on her arm. The fairy walked back and forth from elbow to wrist, lost in thought for a few seconds before she rather cartoonishly snapped her fingers as if getting an idea. In a blast of sparkling light, she zoomed like an arrow into the eucalyptus tree—I swear going straight into the trunk like a ghost.

I sat beside Annie, as did Tammy. Allison plopped down cross-legged facing the kid, basically forming a circle with us.

"The monster is gone," I said.

Annie looked up at me, a crack of worry breaking past her happiness.

"No need to be scared." I patted her on the head.

"I destroyed him. He can't ever hurt you again… or anyone else."

She beamed. "Miss Maple told me already. Thank you!"

Other fairies landed on my shoulders. One tap-danced on my head. I shifted my eyes upward as my kids laughed. Oh, this is too strange. I was never the sort of kid who played with dolls, though maybe that happened because I didn't have any. And not to call the fairies dolls, but they do kinda tweak the same sort of impulse. As weird as it was, I found myself adoring their company. Tammy, too, seemed to slide out from under her shell of surliness, acting more like the Tammy from ten years ago.

Though he had zero interest in fairies, Anthony, standing some twenty feet away, still smiled at seeing his sister in good spirits.

Maple reappeared with a loud fizzling *pop*, emerging from the tree trunk. She and two other fairies lugged an amulet over to me. A cabochon of amber a bit bigger than my thumbprint sat in an oval of woven twigs and tiny leaves, suspended by a plain leather cord.

"Thank you…" I accepted the amulet and spent a moment staring at it. Somehow, I could tell it carried a strong fairy enchantment, but couldn't discern its purpose.

When I started to put it on, Maple rapidly shook her head and pointed at Tammy.

Oh? I handed it to my daughter. She gave it a

dubious look, as if to say 'what's up with this cheap costume jewelry,' but put it on anyway. Two seconds later, she covered her mouth with both hands and looked around at us all before bursting into sobs. Maple floated over to her. Tammy forced a "Thank you" past her tears and gingerly hugged the little woman. Since she couldn't *really* hug the fairy, she clamped herself to my arm instead.

Annie and Allison peered quizzically at her.

Maple landed on Annie's shoulder and chattered away too fast for me to understand, perhaps not even in English.

"Oh…" Annie smiled, then looked at me.

Tammy continued blubbing into my shoulder and neck.

"What…?" I rubbed my daughter's back, trying to comfort her.

"You really do have to learn how to talk to fairies someday." Annie grinned. "Maple wanted to do something nice for you because you helped me. She knew what you wanted most and made the necklace for Tammy."

Maple chattered away.

Annie nodded at her, then looked back to me. "When Tammy wears it, it stops her from hearing all those crazy voices."

My eyes widened in shock.

"I forgot what quiet sounded like," sniffled Tammy.

I squeezed her tight, both of us shaking with

emotion. Somehow, Maple had read my deepest want… for my daughter to be safe from her own demons, not to harm herself or lose her mind. The fairy picked that moment to glide closer to me. She hugged my cheek, then nuzzled against the side of my head like an affectionate mouse.

Words failed me as I was too choked up to speak. It didn't matter though, since Maple sensed my gratitude for her wonderful gift.

Eventually, both Tammy and I regained our composure. We spent a little while longer talking to Annie. She explained, basically translating for Maple, that my daughter could overpower the amulet to use her telepathy on a single person close enough to see. However, she'd have to take it off to do any beyond-line-of-sight stuff or hear/affect multiple minds at once.

Tammy jokingly commented about getting the amulet remade into a collar with a lock so it would never come off, though she sighed and admitted she might need to use her more far-reaching abilities… especially with Elizabeth still out there. However, since the amulet offered her a reprieve from the constant barrage of information, opening herself to the chaos on purpose here and there in small bursts wouldn't bother her at all.

At Annie's parents calling for her, our little fairy conclave meeting broke up. We walked with the girl back to the house and spent a few minutes telling Rita and Gene about the destruction of the

Red Rider.

And... it was time to go home.

Once we piled back into the Momvan, I glanced over my shoulder at Allison and the kids. "You guys wanna swing by the mall real quick on the way? I'm still a bit hungry."

The kids laughed.

Allison gave me a look like I'd suggested we do something naughty. "Ooh. Perfect opportunity to practice controlling it."

"I think I'm figuring this energy thing out pretty quick. I didn't siphon anything from Annie, or you guys even though I'm still kinda hungry."

"Well, if you were at the point of starving before," said Kingsley, "your subconscious might've taken over and done what was necessary for self-preservation. It is possible that under normal circumstances—i.e., not starving—you'd have to actively want to absorb nourishment."

"Great. Good an excuse as any to go to the mall. I still need to do more testing."

"On?" asked Allison.

"Not sure if my telepathy or mind control powers are still there."

"You're not going to make that donation guy sing Figaro again, are you?" asked Tammy.

I cackled. "Oh, I wouldn't dream of it."

25.

Well, I learned a few things at the mall.

One, a giant crowd is basically a buffet. Within five minutes of walking down the concourse, I felt like I'd overdone it on food. Taking tiny scraps of mental energy from a hundred different people was ridiculously easy, unnoticeable, and it tasted *way* better than cow or pig blood.

To be truthful, it didn't really *taste* like anything. Which, given the rancid flavor of blood, I considered an improvement. Instead of flavor, this psychic vampirism deal was more like going from hungry to full over the course of a minute or five without any true sensation of consumption or taste.

I did experiment with eating normal food. It seemed that Talos' opinion that my creator-ness pushing my wants into some sort of reality held true. I didn't feel like throwing up what I ate, even with the ring off. Perhaps because I no longer counted as an undead? I *had* missed food more than almost anything else about being alive. Though, I can't say that food offered me any real nutrition. Though maybe it did. I didn't really know. Considering I needed to absorb mental energy from others now instead of blood, I doubted any other nourishment really worked for me. Which meant I could still eat a hot fudge sundae loaded with brownie chunks without any guilt at all.

Yeah, life was good.

Between the inter-dimensional hopping, our fight with the Red Rider, and puking up an ancient sorceress of doom, my exhausted ass spent a few days loafing around the house trying to avoid people. Allison came by to visit and we did some witchy type stuff. According to her, I *had* magic, but didn't have much of any clue how to tap into it. She said I was as strong as I should've been had nothing weird happened during this lifetime. Maybe even stronger since this lifetime is going to be the last one for me. She's made it her new mission in life to work with me, and seemed as thrilled as a giddy schoolgirl about it.

She still hadn't lowered her mental shield, even though she trusted me and knew Elisabeth was gone. Evidently, she needed the okay from Millicent first.

Anyway, a few days after normality returned—

or at least the best that passed for normality in my life at this point—I started making phone calls and dealing with that whole inherited creepy-as-hell mansion thing.

I can't say I felt any temptation at all to move into that place. Tammy and Anthony agreed on that point. Neither of them liked the vibe of the house nor did I want to uproot them from their school and friends. So, I decided to sell the place. Money was good, and something I didn't have anywhere near enough of. Plus the property taxes on a place like that would be astronomical.

Rather than go through the usual channels, I figured I'd try niche markets first. I got lucky… the first person I contacted about it, Fang, almost did a backflip at the thought. Apparently, his blood bank business was doing pretty good. Then again, we were talking *a lot* of money here. Whatever secret some vampires had to generate cash out of thin air somehow eluded me. Maybe it *was* that whole power of wanting thing. I've never craved being wealthy, just having enough to survive. Though after 'just surviving' for years, it will be nice to be comfortable.

Oh, and Mary Lou did a good impression of a demon-possessed hamster on a partial overdose of amphetamines when I told her everything that happened. I almost needed to mentally compel her to calm down, but she managed it on her own. I can't say whether she was more excited for me or dreading what Elizabeth would do now that she'd gotten off the leash so to speak. I countered by saying if what she'd told me was true, she had never truly been on any leash at all... merely using me the way people use cars.

***

Four days after destroying the Red Rider, I headed out to the house after sunset to meet Fang and a realtor I'd hired to deal with the paperwork. The bizarre old couple showed us around. Despite the outward appearance of needing some work, and the inward overabundance of creep, Fang adored it. Speaking of adored, I adored no longer feeling like a prisoner of the night. Probably why I had spent so many years going to great lengths to defy the sun however possible. But, hey, the big ball of fire and I have made up and we're friends again. Now I just need to find someone interested in a fifty-gallon drum of sunscreen.

Maybe I'll even visit the beach again soon... though Tammy's so pale, if she went outside in a bathing suit she'd probably blind pilots from the glare. Having a vampire mama tended to result in a lot of 'indoor time' for me and the kids.

We ran into the shadow beings during our walkthrough, and it reminded me of the promise I'd made to help free them back in the boxing gym.

"Oops," I said to the shadow watching me.

"Sorry, it took me so long to come back here. I got sidetracked with something on a bit of a time limit."

It nodded solemnly. Then again, I think everything this creature did, it did solemnly.

"So, umm… how do I free you guys?"

The shadow grasped at its chest and thrust its arm forward.

"I have to rip my heart out?"

It shook its head and made a series of gestures. Ugh. I've always hated charades. This poor creature is harder to interpret than my father after six joints and a case of Budweiser.

"Hang on." I stepped closer to it, leaving Fang, my realtor, and Fang's realtor to wander off together exploring. "Let me try something."

The shadow figure hung there like a soot-stained bit of cobweb with eyes.

It almost had readable thoughts, though they flitted around, collapsing in on themselves before blooming again further away from me. Attempting to discern them amounted to trying to pick up raw eggs with my bare hands. However, I picked up enough to suggest whatever force bound them here obeyed the current master of the house. Also, he wanted freedom or oblivion, not to possess anyone or cause harm. No guarantee he'd stay benign after release, since those in captivity often had desperate thoughts.

But… I did give my word back in the gym.

As far as the shadow figure knew, I merely had

to collect the floating candles from the corridors that served as wards to block them in. He trailed after me as I made the rounds, grabbing candle after candle. Once I plucked the thirteenth one out of the air and added it to the stack, he bowed, spread his arms, and disappeared in a shimmer that I now recognized to mean he'd gone up to a different dimension.

Well, there's that. Guess he wasn't lying. He won't be causing any trouble in this world.

I waited a moment for the others to leave, then re-hung the floating candles where they'd been. The house might need whatever protection they afforded as they could easily have been keeping other things *out*.

That done, I made my way toward the sound of voices. Fang and the two realtors stood in the enormous kitchen. The agents discussed the particulars of the sale while Fang chatted up the old couple, evidently adoring them. Seems I made a good decision to ask him about the place.

My phone rang within seconds of inserting myself into their conversation.

"Ugh. Hang on." I pulled it out and answered. "Hello?"

"Sam… we need to talk," said Max… or Archibald Maximus, the alchemist.

Uh oh. I didn't like the tone in his voice. It made me feel too much like a kid in trouble. Or maybe that came from my guilty conscience.

"Okay. I'll be right there. Just need to wrap up a quick thing here."

"All right. This is important."

"I understand, Max. How urgent is it?"

"Tomorrow is fine."

After hanging up, I spent another few hours with the realtors and Fang, and we shook hands on a verbal commitment to do the deal. The paperwork would take weeks, but we'd gotten the ball rolling.

***

Speaking of change... you know what feels *super* bizarre? Sleeping at night.

Whatever I've become, I'm not beholden to a nocturnal schedule anymore. I still evidently require sleep, but ever since my experience outside the third dimension, I've been waking up after only four-ish hours. I still don't dream, and as soon as I make a deliberate effort to go to sleep, it's exactly like my vampiric rest had been—zonk straight out.

Since I've apparently decided to wake up early now, I'd gotten back into the habit of fixing an actual breakfast for the kids. They've been unsure how to handle me wide awake in the morning. Ever since they'd been tiny, they've had to deal with me being barely coherent before late afternoon. For most of their lives, me forcing myself up and about during the day resulted in my being more or less a high-functioning zombie.

Once they were off to school, I hurried out the door for my meeting with Max. I'd say anxiety over this meeting had something to do with me only getting four hours of sleep, but I don't think my sleep works that way anymore.

***

I strolled into the library, cringing at the overwhelming darkness in the air around the books.

Yeah, they'd felt bad before, but the chilling doom they threw off seemed far more intense. I suspected that without Elizabeth inside my head, the energy in them viewed me as hostile, or at least as a complete stranger. Maybe, too, since I'd regained body heat and my heart now worked like it should, I'd become more sensitive to evil of this magnitude. It's difficult to give a corpse a chill after all. Also, I knew she'd been responsible for binding some of the entities within the books, which might account for why they no longer called out to me.

Thank God...

Archibald Maximus strolled urgently over. For an instant, I expected him to grab me by the arms and give me a verbal lashing for doing something bad, but when he reached me, he simply stared at me with an expression as though I'd run over his dog and laughed about it.

"Oh, this can't be good," I said. "Whatever it is."

"You don't know?" He blinked.

"Evidently not… though maybe I have some suspicions."

"Why don't you tell me what you think you know and I'll fill in the rest?" He paced around, hands in his pockets, his ever-changing eyes—this time they were gray—flashing.

I explained what happened with the Red Rider, visiting the 99th dimension, and barfing out Elizabeth.

He nodded along as though none of what I said surprised him. At least until I got to the part about my no longer being an undead and evidently having regained the magic I'd been destined to inherit in this reincarnation. When I reached out a hand so he could check my fingernails, he took it gently, studying me like a jeweler.

"Amazing… but I'm afraid things are far worse than you imagined."

I blinked. "I seriously hope you're not about to tell me I'm going to die in a few years or something."

"No. I'm certain you are still as immortal as you were before, for your soul is still fully contained within your corporeal form. Indeed, Father Time is no threat to you, but other things are. They're a threat, well, to everything."

"Uh oh. Did I do something bad?"

"Yes." He sighed. "But, you had no idea. She played on your compassion. And, she had me fooled as well, so I can't fault you. While I'm sure my mother had no control over that Red Rider, she knew he would eventually reach a point of starvation where he would begin preying on children."

"He preyed on children the whole time," I snapped, a little nastier than I meant to. "Sixteen is still a child."

"Yes, yes, but a ten-year-old angered you beyond reason. By destroying him and releasing magic back into the world, you inadvertently gave my mother the means to break down the barriers of the Void. All the Dark Masters that had been imprisoned in there will soon be free… and they're in the process of doing what my mother did... manifesting into their own bodies."

"Ah, shit." I flinched, only half contrite. No way could I have allowed Annie to die, especially such a torturous death.

Max bowed his head. "I am not upset with you. I'm upset that Elizabeth and her underlings are free from the Void."

"I had no idea… I merely destroyed a source of incalculable evil."

"My mother knew you. She knew everything about you. The Red Rider preyed on children. What wounds your heart more than anything? People who harm kids. While you *did* do the world a great service, you have unwittingly unleashed…" He let off a heavy sigh. "We're in for a war, Sam. It's going to get nasty."

"How long do we have?"

"It will take my mother some time to gather power. A few years... maybe as many as ten. Maybe as few as one. Considering how patient she had been to let her plan play out, I imagine she will not be rushing into anything. She made that mistake once."

"What happened?"

"She wound up in the Void."

"What of the other creatures of the world? The werewolves and mermaids and even the Lichtenstein monsters? Will their dark masters flee their hosts, as well?"

"I doubt they can. They knew the consequences of taking possession early on, leading the charge so to speak. But that does not mean they are happy with it. Undoubtedly, some will do all they can to end the lives of their hosts."

I nodded. "Freeing them to take their own form again."

"Indeed, Sam."

"And what of those who are, you know, happy with the current set up?" I knew, for instance, that Kingsley had an agreement with the entity within him. He fed the bastard rotten meat each month, and in turn, the entity left him alone. Kingsley also spoke once or twice of his past mermaid wife who'd had a real friendship with her dark master.

Maximus read my thoughts like a pro. "The mermaid of which you speak is known to me, as are others of her kind. Many host dark masters from another epoch, another set of circumstances, and they have no dog in my mother's fight. I understand you have several close immortal friends. Watch them, Samantha. They are in danger."

"And the only way for such dark masters to leave a host is through death?"

"Precisely. In your case, the blast of magic did the job. Few will ever come across such conditions again."

I didn't know much about the dark master inside Fang. Perhaps my friend could strike a deal with the guy... give him what he wants within reason. But, I guess, that also meant Fang would join sides with Elizabeth. Or he could just remain strong and...

"Vigilant," added Max. "I see in your mind's eye that the one you call Fang has allowed his dark master to temporarily take him over. A poor decision. It wouldn't be very difficult for his dark master, in full control of Fang's body, to drive a silver dagger into his heart. Indeed, your friend is in grave danger."

"Unless his dark master wants nothing to do with the coming war."

"There's always that chance."

"But it's doubtful," I added glumly.

"My mother and her cohort Cornelius have promised their followers immortality... and so far have delivered. In return, they demand loyalty."

"War huh…" I glanced at the shelves of dark

books, then at my pinkish hands. They had color now. *Color.* "Count me in."

Max offered a wan smile. "I'd have expected nothing less from you."

"Oh did you notice anything?" I leaned closer to him, showing off my face.

He studied me for a few seconds, then subtly shook his head. Of course, being his mother's son, he was arguably the second or third strongest telepath and could have read my mind. But he didn't out of common courtesy. Or didn't let on that he had.

"A suntan." I smiled, despite my nervousness at the coming storm.

"Looks good on you, Samantha Moon. You know, I can't say I've ever encountered a being such as you."

"I'm special like that."

A warm smile finally broke through his gloom. "A true angel."

"Nah." I winked. "Only about a quarter."

The End

To be continued in:
Dead Moon
Vampire for Hire #17
Coming soon!

About the Authors:

J.R. Rain is an ex-private investigator who now writes full-time. He lives in a small house on a small island with his small dog, Sadie. Please visit him at www.jrrain.com.

~~~~~

Matthew S. Cox has been creating science fiction and fantasy worlds for most of his reasoning life. Since 1996, he has developed the "Divergent Fates" world, in which Division Zero, Virtual Immortality, The Awakened Series, The Harmony Paradox, and the Daughter of Mars series take place.

Matthew is an avid gamer, a recovered WoW addict, Gamemaster for two custom systems, and a fan of anime, British humour, and intellectual science fiction that questions the nature of reality, life, and what happens after it.

He is also fond of cats.

Please visit him at www.matthewcoxbooks.com.

Printed in Great Britain
by Amazon